~Presents~

Take time out from your busy schedule this month to kick back and relax with a brand-new Harlequin Presents novel. We hope you enjoy this month's selection.

If you love royal heroes, you're in for a treat this month! In Penny Jordan's latest book, *The Italian Duke's Wife,* an Italian aristocrat chooses a young English woman as his convenient wife. When he unleashes within her a desire she never knew she possessed, he is soon regretting his no-consummation rule.... Emma Darcy's sheikh in *Traded to the Sheikh* is an equally powerful and sexy alpha male. This story has a wonderfully exotic desert setting, too!

We have some gorgeous European men this month. *Shackled by Diamonds* by Julia James is part of our popular miniseries GREEK TYCOONS. Read about a Greek tycoon and the revenge he plans to exact on an innocent, beautiful model when he wrongly suspects her of stealing his priceless diamonds. In Sarah Morgan's *Public Wife, Private Mistress,* can a passionate Italian's marriage be rekindled when he is unexpectedly reunited with his estranged wife?

In *The Antonides Marriage Deal* by Anne McAllister, a Greek magnate meets a stunning new business partner, and he begins to wonder if he can turn their business arrangement into a permanent contract—such as marriage! Kay Thorpe's *Bought by a Billionaire* tells of a Portuguese billionaire and his ex-lover. He wants her back as his mistress. Previously she rejected his proposal because of his arrogance and his powerful sexuality. But this time he wants marriage....

Happy reading! Look out for a brand-new selection next month.

Harlequin Presents®

ITALIAN HUSBANDS

They're tall, dark…and ready to marry!

If you love reading about our sensual Italian men,
don't delay, look out for the next story
in this great miniseries!

Sarah Morgan

PUBLIC WIFE, PRIVATE MISTRESS

ITALIAN HUSBANDS

HARLEQUIN®

TORONTO • NEW YORK • LONDON
AMSTERDAM • PARIS • SYDNEY • HAMBURG
STOCKHOLM • ATHENS • TOKYO • MILAN • MADRID
PRAGUE • WARSAW • BUDAPEST • AUCKLAND

ISBN 0-373-12532-1

PUBLIC WIFE, PRIVATE MISTRESS

First North American Publication 2006.

This edition published by arrangement with Harlequin Books S.A.

® and TM are trademarks of the publisher. Trademarks indicated with ® are registered in the United States Patent and Trademark Office, the Canadian Trade Marks Office and in other countries.

www.eHarlequin.com

Printed in U.S.A.

All about the author...
Sarah Morgan

SARAH MORGAN was born in Wiltshire and started writing at the age of eight when she produced an autobiography of her hamster.

At the age of eighteen she traveled to London to train as a nurse in one of London's top teaching hospitals, and she describes what happened in those years as extremely happy and definitely censored!

She worked in a number of areas after she qualified, but her favorite was A&E, where she found the work stimulating and fun. Nowhere else in the hospital environment did she encounter such good teamwork between doctors and nurses.

Her first completed manuscript, written after the birth of her first child, was rejected, but the comments were encouraging, so she tried again; on the third attempt her manuscript *Worth the Risk* was accepted unchanged. She describes receiving the acceptance letter as one of the best moments of her life, after meeting her husband and having her two children.

Sarah still works part-time in a health-related industry and spends the rest of the time with her family trying to squeeze in writing whenever she can. She is an enthusiastic skier and walker, and loves outdoor life.

CHAPTER ONE

SHE was *not* going to die.

Rico Crisanti, billionaire President of the Crisanti Corporation, stared grimly through the window that separated the relatives' room from the intensive care unit, oblivious to the dreamy stares of the nurses working on the unit. He was used to women staring. Women always stared. Sometimes he noticed. Sometimes he didn't.

Today he didn't.

His gaze was fixed on the still body of the girl who lay on the bed, surrounded by doctors and high-tech machinery.

The jacket of his designer suit had long since been removed, tossed with careless disregard for its future appearance over the back of a standard issue hospital chair, and he now stood in a state of rigid tension, silk shirtsleeves rolled back to reveal bronzed forearms, his firm jaw grazed by a dark stubble that made him more bandit than businessman.

For a man as driven as Rico, a man accustomed to controlling and directing, *a man accustomed to action*, the waiting was proving to be the worst kind of torture.

Waiting for anything was *not* his strong point.

He wanted the problem fixed now. But for the first time in his life he'd discovered that there was something that he couldn't control. Something that money couldn't buy.

The life of his teenage sister.

Rico swore softly under his breath, fighting the temptation to punch his fist through the glass.

He'd been at the hospital for the best part of two weeks and *never* had he felt so helpless. Never had he felt so ill-equipped to solve a problem that confronted him.

Blocking out the muted sobs of his mother, grandmother, aunt and two cousins, he stared in brooding, frustrated silence at the still figure, as if the very force of his personality might be sufficient to rouse her from her unconscious state.

There must be something more he could do. He was the man with a solution for everything and he *refused* to give up.

He sucked in a breath and tried to think clearly, but he'd recently discovered that lack of sleep, grief and worry were not a combination designed to focus the mind. Fear had induced a mind-numbing paralysis that was becoming harder to shake with each passing hour.

Trying to clear his head, he inhaled deeply and ran a hand over the back of his neck, clenching his jaw as his mother gave another poorly disguised sob of distress. The sound cut like a blade through his heart. The expectation of his family weighed on him heavily and for the first time in his life he knew what it felt like to be truly helpless.

He'd flown in a top neurosurgeon who had operated to relieve the pressure on Chiara's brain caused by the bleed. She was breathing on her own but still hadn't recovered consciousness. Her life hung in the balance and no one could predict the outcome. No one could answer the question.

Life or death.

And if it were life, would it be life with disability,

or life as Chiara had known it before the horse had thrown her?

He swore softly and raked strong fingers through his hair. To Rico, that was the hardest aspect to cope with. The exquisite, drawn out mental torture of waiting. He'd seen his mother worn down by it, had watched the black shadows grow under her eyes as she lived under the cruel shadow of uncertainty on a daily basis. *Had watched her wither slightly as she was forced to ask herself whether this would be the day when she lost her only daughter—*

Suddenly his own powerlessness mocked him and had he not been too drained for laughter, then he would have laughed at his own arrogance.

Had he really thought that he could control destiny?

The vow he'd made to his father, the vow he'd made to look after the family, seemed suddenly empty and worthless. What did it matter that he'd created an empire from nothing but dust using only fierce determination? What did it matter that his success in building that empire had been nothing short of staggering? Somewhere along the way he'd started to believe that there was nothing he couldn't control. Nothing he couldn't do if he set his mind to it. And it had taken this accident to remind him that no amount of riches could protect a man from the hand of fate.

Driven by the monumental frustration of doing nothing, he loosened another button on his silk shirt with impatient fingers and paced the room, his long strides and the confined space combining to provide little in the way of relief. Emotion, as unwelcome as it was unfamiliar, clogged his throat and for the first time since he was a small child he felt the hot sting of tears threaten his usually icy composure.

Cursing his own weakness, he closed his eyes and rubbed long fingers along the bridge of his nose as if he could physically hold back the building pressure of grief.

It would help no one if he crumbled.

The whole family was on the edge, grasping on to fragile threads of hope extended by grim-faced doctors. His was the strength that they used. The rock that they leaned on. If he caved in, gave in to the desire to howl like a baby, then the morale of the whole family would disintegrate. The game they were playing—the game of hope—would be ended.

So instead he stared in brooding silence at the bruised, immobile body of his sister, willing her to wake up, and he was still staring when the door opened again, this time to admit the doctor who was in charge of his sister's case together with several more junior doctors.

Ignoring the minions and the immediate response of his own security team to this latest intrusion, Rico's attention zeroed in on the man in charge, sensing from his manner that he had news to impart. Suddenly he was almost afraid to ask the question that needed to be asked.

'Any change?' His voice was hoarse with strain, lack of sleep and something much worse. The fear of prompting bad news. 'Has there been any change?'

'Some.' The doctor cleared his throat, clearly more than a little intimidated by the formidable status of the man standing in front of him. 'Her vital signs have improved slightly and she regained consciousness briefly,' he announced quietly. 'She spoke.'

'She spoke?' Relief flooded through him and for the first time in days he felt lighter. 'She said something?'

The doctor nodded. 'She was very difficult to under-

stand, but one of the nurses thinks that it was a name.'
He hesitated and looked at them questioningly. 'Stasia?
It sounded like Stasia. Could that be right?'

Stasia?

Rico froze, momentarily stunned into shocked silence, while behind him his mother gave a strangled
gasp of horror and his grandmother gave another wail.

Rico gritted his teeth and tried to shut out the sound.
He would have done anything to banish his well-
meaning family to the privacy of his estate but he knew
that, for the time being, that option was out of the question. They needed to be here with Chiara. It was just
unfortunate that their hysterical display of emotion was
making his job harder, not easier.

And now that Stasia had been mentioned the situation
was about to deteriorate rapidly.

The mere sound of her name was enough to detonate
an explosion within his family.

And as for his own feelings—

He closed his eyes briefly and rubbed long fingers
over his bronzed forehead. With his sister fighting for
her life, he didn't need to be thinking about Stasia. It
seemed that fate was determined to make further efforts
to crush him.

The doctor cleared his throat. 'Well, whoever she
is—could she be brought to the hospital?'

Ignoring his mother's moan of denial, Rico forced
himself to focus on the main issue. His sister's recovery.
Somehow he voiced the words. 'Would it make a difference?'

'It might.' The doctor shrugged. 'Difficult to say, but
anything is worth a try. Can she be contacted?'

Not without considerable emotional sacrifice.

His mother rose to her feet, her face contorting with anger and pain. 'No! I won't have her here! She—'

'Enough!' Rico felt the ripple of curiosity spread through the medical team and silenced his mother with one cool, quelling flash of his unusually expressive black eyes.

It was bad enough that the world's press was camped on their doorstep, tracking every moment of their darkest hour, without supplying them with further fodder for gossip.

Stasia.

How ironic that this should happen now, he reflected, when the connection between them was about to be severed permanently. He had thought that there was no circumstance that would ever require him to lay eyes on his wife again. For the past few months he'd had a team of lawyers working overtime to draw up a divorce settlement that he thought was fair. Enough to buy her out of his life and leave him with a clear conscience to marry again. This time to a gentle, compliant Italian girl who understood what it meant to be the wife of a traditional Italian male.

Not a fiery English redhead who was all heat and spark and knew *nothing* about compliance.

He sucked in a breath as a clear vision of Stasia—*wild, beautiful Stasia*—flared in his mind and he felt the immediate throb of raw sexual heat pulse through his body. It had been a year since their final, blistering encounter and despite the distasteful circumstances of their parting, his body still craved her with almost indecent desperation. *And he didn't trust himself to see her again.* She affected his judgement in ways that he didn't want to admit, even to himself.

Despite everything she'd done, Stasia was as addictive as any drug and seeing her again was *not* a sensible move. In the past year he'd learned to hate her, had learned to see her for what she was.

A mistake.

Rico paced back to the window and studied his sister in brooding silence, an ominous expression on his handsome face as he reviewed his options. They were depressingly limited. Reaching the unpalatable conclusion that his own needs and wishes had to be secondary to the issue of his sister's recovery, he forced himself to accept that he was going to have to see Stasia again.

He'd fully intended to end the entire fiasco of their marriage through lawyers and there was no reason why this couldn't still happen, he assured himself swiftly. This was just a temporary stasis in proceedings. He could fly her out and she could do whatever needed to be done and then he could have her flown home again.

It was entirely possible that they could avoid all but the briefest of conversations. Which would suit him perfectly. He had no desire whatsoever to indulge in any reminiscence of the past. *And even less desire to spend time with the woman.*

He gave a grim smile, knowing that the irony of the situation wouldn't be lost on Stasia. Dazzling, unconventional Stasia. The woman who had never conformed to his family's perceptions of the perfect Sicilian wife.

Or his.

He'd given her *everything*. Had done everything a husband should do. And still, apparently, it had not been enough.

The doctor cleared his throat discreetly and Rico stirred, making the only decision that he was in a position to make.

'I will send for her.' He turned to Gio, his head of

security. 'Contact her and make arrangements for her to be flown out immediately.'

He caught the startled glance of the man who'd known him from childhood, heard the shocked gasp of his mother and gritted his teeth as he battled to come to terms with the fact that he was going to have to do the one thing he'd promised himself that he'd never have to do again. Come face to face with Stasia.

One day soon he was going to put her behind him, he vowed. One day soon he'd be able to think of her without feeling an instantaneous reaction in every male part of himself. And the sooner that day came the better.

Anastasia put the finishing touches to the painting, stepped back with her eyes narrowed and gave a nod of satisfaction.

Finally. Finally it was ready.

Mark would be pleased.

With a final glance at the canvas, she cleaned her brush and then wandered out of her studio into the kitchen, flicking on the kettle and reaching for a pile of post that had been accumulating over the past two weeks while she'd been concentrating on her painting.

Still leafing through her post, she reached across to switch on her mobile and it rang immediately.

Knowing that it would be her mother, she answered the phone with a smile. 'How's business?'

'Business is booming.' Her mother sounded excited. And confident. Miles removed from the terrified, mouse-like woman she'd been, after Stasia's father had walked out with a blonde half his age, six years earlier.

Stasia gritted her teeth, trying not to remember that awful time. She'd been in her first year at university and if ever she'd needed evidence that depending on a man, any man, was not a good idea, she'd been given it in spades. Her mother had relied on her father for everything, and when he left she'd been totally unable to cope. Had lost all belief in herself.

It had been Stasia who had pointed out that her mother knew a great deal about antiques. Stasia who had helped her put that knowledge to commercial use by opening a small antiques business. Gradually the word had spread and soon her mother wasn't just selling antiques, she was advising clients on furnishing entire houses. And six months ago, thanks to a generous business loan, they'd expanded their premises and business was booming.

'We're going to have to employ more help, Stasia,' her mother was saying briskly. 'I need to go on a buying trip and I've been invited to a stately home in Yorkshire to advise on restoring some of their antiques and obviously I can't just close the shop. People travel from all over the country to visit. It wouldn't be fair on them if we closed. And you're too busy painting to help.'

Stasia smiled. It was wonderful to hear her mother so animated. 'You're running the show, Mum,' she said lightly, throwing a pile of junk mail into the bin. 'Employ away. The painting is finished, by the way. Mark can collect it whenever he likes.'

'Marvellous. I'll tell him, if I see him before you do. And how are you, darling? Are you eating?'

'Yes.' It was a lie. She hadn't done much eating at all in the last year. Since leaving Italy, her emotions had been so disrupted that eating no longer seemed important. But she didn't want her mother to worry. 'I'm fine, Mum. Truly.'

Her mother sighed. 'Which means you're still pining after that Sicilian.' Her voice took on a hard edge. 'Take it from me, Stasia, men like him never change. I should know. I lived with your father for all those years and he was exactly the same. I was just a possession and when he got bored with me he purchased something new.'

Stasia heard a car negotiating the potholes in the lane outside the cottage and snatched at the excuse to end the conversation. 'I can't talk now, Mum—I've got a visitor. It's probably Mark about the painting. I'll call you later.'

Without giving her mother time to protest, she hung up and switched off the phone, releasing a long breath. She adored her mother but that was one conversation she wasn't prepared to have with anyone.

The car came to a halt and Stasia pulled a face. She didn't really want to see Mark. He made no secret of the fact that he wanted more from her than her paintings and she wasn't ready for that. Maybe she never would be.

Glancing down at her paint-spattered jeans, she gave a rueful smile. She looked a mess. But if Mark insisted on dropping in without phoning first, what could he expect?

Anticipating the knock before it came, she opened her front door and froze in shock as she saw who stood there.

Rico Crisanti.

Billionaire and bastard.

The last person in the world she'd expected to see.

Her heart lurched, the whole world tilted, and for a wild, ecstatic minute she thought he'd finally come after her. And then reality struck and she remembered that it had been a year and that he was in the process of divorcing her. Which could only mean that he was here for an entirely different reason. And, whatever it was, she wasn't interested.

'No!' Her immediate impulse to slam the door in his face was thwarted by swift action on his part. Clearly he'd anticipated her response to his arrival and in a powerful movement he slammed a hand in the centre of the door, resisting her attempts to close it.

'You don't answer your mail and you don't have a phone,' he launched savagely, dark eyes connecting with hers with the lethal force of a missile, 'and you bury yourself in a place so remote that it is almost impossible to find you.'

'And it didn't occur to you that maybe I didn't *want* you to find me? If I'd wanted you to find me then I would have left a forwarding address.' She glared at him, previous hostilities rising to the surface with such frightening force and speed that for a moment she struggled to breathe, swept away on a tide of emotion. 'And if I'd thought there was *any* chance at all that you'd even look for me then I would have buried myself even deeper,' she shot back hoarsely, suddenly wishing she'd done just that.

But it had never entered her head that he'd come after her. Not after those first miserable months where she'd done nothing but stare out of the window, desperately hoping to see one of his flashy sports cars pull up outside wherever she was living. Gradually she'd grown accustomed to the knowledge that he wasn't coming after her.

That it was well and truly over. Ended with an explosion of bitter emotion every bit as intense as the fiery relationship that had gone before. She'd walked out. He hadn't followed. And that had said everything there was to say about their short, fragile marriage. To him it hadn't been worth saving. It had been an unmitigated disaster and she'd already promised herself that if she *ever* fell in love again it would be with a safe, mild-mannered, modern Englishman, *not* a blisteringly ruth-less, own-the-world Sicilian whose attitude to women was firmly embedded in the Stone Age. Who thought that the answer to everything was money.

She stared at him furiously, her gaze drawn by the power of his broad shoulders, the arrogant tilt of his handsome head and the dangerous glint in his cold, hard eyes. It was wrong for one man to be so indecently sexy, she thought numbly, trying valiantly to ignore the kick of her heart and the sudden quickening of her pulse. She didn't want to respond like this. It was this response that had involved her with him in the first place.

Against her better judgement.

But Rico Crisanti was not a man that women ignored. He was indecently good-looking and the aura of power that he wore with the ease of a designer suit attracted women like sharks to blood-infested water.

And she'd proved as vulnerable to his particular brand of macho Sicilian sex appeal as all the others.

Suddenly aware that he was staring over her shoulder into her cottage, she saw the flicker of surprise cross his handsome face and had a wild and totally inappro-priate impulse to laugh. Rico Crisanti, Italian billionaire and business tycoon, owned six homes around the world and had probably never been anywhere remotely like her tiny cottage. At another time she would have teased him about it, but they were way beyond teasing.

The differences in their attitudes and approach to life were so far apart that nothing could bridge them. He believed that a woman's place was at home, waiting for her man, whereas she wanted to get out of the home, grab life by the throat and rattle it hard.

He was frowning, night-black eyes glittering with a mixture of incredulity and amazement. 'What *is* this place?'

The desire to laugh vanished. 'My *home*, Rico,' she said stiffly. 'And you're not welcome in it.' She didn't need the reminder that he'd never even seen the cottage that she loved so much. *That despite their marriage he knew so little about her. Knew so little about the things that mattered to her—*

She made another futile attempt to close the door, knowing that it was a waste of time. In a battle of strength she would be the loser. Rico Crisanti was six foot three and powerfully built. Even without looking, she knew that somewhere close by would be a car full of bodyguards. Their constant presence had always amused her because no one with reasonable vision could ever doubt that Rico could handle himself physically if required to do so. He was an expert in martial arts, supremely fit, with the body and the stamina of an Olympic athlete. But the billionaire President of one of the most successful companies in the Western world was a prime target for corporate kidnapping and extortion and he had no intention of making access to him easy.

Stasia subdued a hysterical laugh.

If he was kidnapped then it would mean taking a day off work, and that would be more challenging for Rico Crisanti than any form of torture.

The man was driven.

He couldn't function without work and she'd loved to tease him about that fact. On one occasion she'd even hidden his mobile phone and he'd gone ballistic—until he'd discovered exactly *where* she'd hidden it.

She lifted her chin, trying not to remember those early ecstatic days of their relationship. Before reality had set in. Before they'd discovered that they had absolutely nothing in common. 'So how *did* you find me?'

'With considerable difficulty and much personal inconvenience,' he bit out harshly. 'And already I have wasted too much time. My pilot is refuelling as we speak. We need to be back in the air within the hour.'

Stasia gaped at him with the same blank astonishment with which he'd assessed her cottage. His pilot was refuelling? They needed to be in the air within an hour? What exactly was he saying?

'We?' She shook her head and gave a humourless laugh. 'I presume you're using the royal "we." You can't possibly mean you and me.'

They hadn't even spoken for a year. *Not since that night—*

He'd accused her. Matching his temper, burn for burn, she'd walked out without even bothering to defend herself, so angry with him that she hadn't trusted herself to speak. Hadn't trusted herself not to do him physical damage.

If she'd needed further evidence that they just couldn't live together, that they were just too different, then she'd had it that night. And if a small part of her had secretly hoped he'd come after her—*fight for their relationship*—then that part of her had soon been disappointed.

They hadn't seen each other since. He'd seen and he'd judged. End of story.

'In my vocabulary "we" means you and I,' he snapped impatiently, 'and, despite your constant digs about my lifestyle, I have *never* had delusions of grandeur.'

That may probably be true, she conceded, and yet in Sicily and Italy he was treated like royalty.

It had been another one of their shared jokes—Cinderella and the Prince.

But neither of them was joking now.

Why would he possibly want her to go anywhere with him?

They both knew that she wasn't what he wanted in a wife.

And yet here he was, standing in her doorway, his broad shoulders almost obliterating the light. And it wouldn't have surprised her to discover that Rico could control night and day. He had control over almost everything else. He was a man who led while others followed.

And something had led him to her door.

'I can't imagine what possessed you to come here when you know full well that I'd never agree to go anywhere with you again. I gave up being a groupie a year ago.'

Had given up being a slave to sex, because that had been the only level on which they had truly connected. Whatever else had gone wrong between them, the sex had always been amazing.

Instead of the incisive retort she'd been expecting, a tense silence followed her declaration. Anticipating the usual verbal sparring, Stasia braced herself and then registered the tension in his broad shoulders and the signs of strain stamped on his flawless features. With a sudden feeling of unease, she realized that he looked tired. And Rico Crisanti was never tired. He had more stamina than anyone she'd ever met. He'd frequently kept her awake all night only to leap out of bed at dawn to attend a business meeting, leaving her to sleep off the sex-induced exhaustion brought on by a night of continual love-making.

Something was very wrong.

She glanced behind him and noticed his driver and two bodyguards that she didn't recognize.

She frowned. 'Where's Gio?'

During the brief period of their marriage, she'd grown fond of Rico's head of security and she knew that he was much more than an employee to Rico. A fellow Sicilian who had known Rico from birth, Gio was frank and straightforward and was rarely far from Rico's side. He'd made Rico's protection and privacy his personal crusade.

'He is at the hospital.' Rico's tone was terse. 'He's the only person I trust to keep the mob at bay.'

His words sank in slowly. 'Hospital?' She frowned. 'Why is he at the hospital? What's happened?'

'Chiara had an accident. She came off her horse.' He delivered that piece of news in clipped tones, his voice displaying not a flicker of emotion. 'She is in a coma. I assumed you would have seen the papers. The story has been everywhere.'

Chiara was in a coma?

'I don't read newspapers any more.' She'd had enough of featuring in newspapers when they had been together and she had every reason to loathe the press. Since they'd parted, she'd stopped reading newspapers of any sort. Stasia stared at him. 'Is she badly injured?'

'*Si.*' He seemed to sag in front of her and she felt a flicker of concern.

She'd never seen Rico like this before. He looked grey. Exhausted. Like a man at the very limit of his reserves. Instinctively she stepped to one side. 'You'd better come in.'

He followed her into the cottage, stooping slightly to avoid banging his head on the door, a frown drawing his ebony brows together as he glanced around him. 'Why are you living like this?' He glanced round him, distaste evident in every angle of his handsome face as he surveyed her tiny sitting room with the one ancient sofa. 'Are you short of money?'

Temporarily forgetting her concern, she felt the anger bubble inside her. With him, everything came down to money. It never occurred to him that she might choose to live in this cottage because she liked it.

'My life is none of your business.' How could she *ever* have fallen in love with a man who was so emotionally stunted? 'You didn't show any interest in it before, so I don't see why you would now.'

'You do *not* need to live like this. You are my wife—'

The ultimate status.

If the pain hadn't been so great she would have laughed. 'I like living like this. And I was *never* your wife, Rico,' she said shakily, brushing aside the fiery red curls that threatened to obscure her vision.

The gesture caught his attention and his shimmering black gaze fixed on her wild mane of hair with almost primal fascination. The tension in the room suddenly increased. For a moment both of them had forgotten Chiara, too absorbed in each other to make room for the pressures of the outside world.

'I married you.'

Clearly he thought it was the biggest honour he could have bestowed on her and she suppressed a bitter laugh.

How could she have forgotten his unshakeable arrogance?

'An impulse that we have both lived to regret.' Stasia wished he'd stop staring at her hair. She recognized that look in his eyes and it was all she could do not to groan out loud. She knew he was seconds away from sliding a possessive hand into her tangled curls and exposing her throat to the heat of his mouth. The seductive stroke of his fingers in her hair had always been a prelude to the most incredible mind-blowing sex. Her breathing quickened. She did *not* want to think about that now! 'It wasn't a marriage in the proper sense. Marriages are about sharing and we never shared anything except sex.'

Incredible, blisteringly exciting sex, the memory of which still deprived her of sleep.

His gaze shifted reluctantly from her hair and settled on her pale face and she knew that his thoughts were running in the same direction as hers. 'I am *not* here to relive every painful moment of our disastrous marriage. But, like it or not, until the divorce is final you are still my wife,' he delivered, his slightly thickened tones betraying his physical response to her. 'As my wife I need you back in Italy. Don't misunderstand me—I have no intention of resurrecting our relationship in any shape or form. This visit isn't personal.'

Pain shafted through her.

Not personal.

She had known that, of course. So why did hearing him state the truth feel so brutal? Why did it hurt so much?

'Of course it isn't personal. Why would I even think that it might be?' Five minutes he'd been in her house. Five minutes and she was ready to scratch and claw until she drew blood. He just made her so *angry*. 'Our marriage was never personal. That was the problem. What we had was legalized sex.'

She heard his sharp intake of breath, saw the streaks of colour appear high on his cheekbones. She could almost taste his own anger. And yet he didn't deny it. How could he when they both knew it was the truth? The sex had been amazing but their relationship had never been any deeper than that. At least, not for him. For her it had been everything.

He was the love of her life.

Which made the whole situation so much more depressing.

'I'm not here to discuss our marriage.' His tone was a cold warning to change the subject and if she hadn't been so miserable and so furious with him she would have laughed at his complete inability to tackle anything emotional.

'Of course you're not. You'd prefer to divorce me without discussion,' she threw back angrily. 'You prefer to communicate through lawyers in sharp suits.'

His anger matched hers. 'You were the one who walked out on our marriage.'

'Because we didn't have a marriage! You didn't trust me! You didn't share with me! Every decision that had to be made, you made it without so much as a flicker of consideration for *my* opinion. And I hardly ever saw you! Which makes it all the more incredible that you're here now when you could have sent one of your minions. It must have been incredibly difficult for you to bring yourself to see me in person.'

His jaw was set hard. 'I'm not afraid of difficult.'

'Then why have you been communicating through lawyers, Rico?'

'*Dio*, this is *not* the time for this discussion!' He

looked at her with blinding hostility, his body language blatantly antagonistic. 'And I'm not asking you to come back to Italy for me. I'm asking you for Chiara.'

The burning anger was rapidly replaced by shame.

She'd forgotten Chiara. How could she have done that? How could being with Rico drive everything else from her mind?

'Naturally I'm sorry she's been injured,' she muttered stiffly, 'but I can't see why you want me in Italy.'

'You are part of the family.'

Astonishment diluted her anger and her mouth fell open. 'You're *seriously* pretending that you want me by your sister's bedside? What is this? A sudden show of family solidarity?' She gave a disbelieving laugh. 'It's a little late for that, Rico.'

She'd *never* been part of his family.

They'd made it clear from the first that they considered her to be a gold-digger, an accusation that should have been utterly laughable given her complete lack of interest in material things. But it hadn't been laughable. It had been tragic. Wrapped up in their own prejudices, they hadn't bothered to get to know her well enough to understand the things that mattered to her. Instead they'd gone out of their way to exclude her. To make her feel like a complete outsider. He'd married her without consulting them—without even inviting them to the wedding—and they'd blamed her for that. To them it had been further proof that she'd married him in a hurry, just to get her hands on his money. She wasn't what they had wanted for Rico and they hadn't been afraid to show it.

He gave a growl like a goaded tiger and his eyes flashed dangerously. '*Madre de Dio.* My sister's life is hanging in the balance and still you malign my family?'

She stilled, shocked by the news that Chiara was so seriously injured. 'She might *die*?' Her voice was a croak and she swallowed hard, suddenly understanding the reason for all the signs of extreme stress that he was displaying. He adored his little sister. 'She is that seriously injured?'

His eyes closed briefly and he let out a breath. 'They told us yesterday that they think she will live, but with what measure of brain damage—' he gave a fatalistic shrug '—they will not know until she wakes up properly. So far she has only uttered a few words.' His expression hardened. 'So you see that your criticism of my family is badly timed.'

'I said nothing bad about your family,' she said tonelessly, quelling her natural desire to defend herself against his accusation. He truly had *no* idea of the true situation. When it came to his family he was utterly blinkered. 'Only about my relationship with them. And I had no idea that Chiara's life was hanging in the balance.'

'She has been in a coma for more than two weeks. She has had brain surgery—'

Genuinely disturbed by that news, Stasia extended a hand in an instinctive gesture of sympathy only to let it fall again as she met those hard, cold eyes.

His look spoke volumes.

Don't touch.

Hands off.

She no longer had the right to deliver comfort of any sort.

Not that Rico Crisanti was a man who expected another's sympathy. He didn't let anyone that close.

Not even his wife.

She withdrew, both physically and mentally, her will

to fight shrivelled by his total indifference to her presence.

Once he hadn't been indifferent. Once he hadn't been able to keep his hands off her. He'd thirsted for her, *starved for her* and his obsession with her had been the biggest aphrodisiac going.

But she wasn't going to think about that now. Thinking about her relationship with Rico would be a fast route to self-destruction. And she really shouldn't care any more. She really *didn't* care.

She lifted her chin and exercised some of the self-control she'd been forced to learn while she had been living with his family. 'I'm truly sorry to hear about Chiara,' she said quietly, 'and of course I'll help in any way I can, but I really can't see why you would want me there.'

Chiara had made it perfectly clear that Stasia wasn't a welcome member of the family.

Rico ran a hand over the back of his neck and drew in a deep breath, as if he were forcing himself to deliver his next statement.

'She has been asking for you—'

Stasia stared at him, her green eyes wide with shock. Of all the things she'd expected him to say, the fact that Chiara had been asking for her had not been among them. 'Chiara *asked* for me? You have to be joking!'

It was the wrong thing to say.

'*Dio*. You, who always accused me of taking life too seriously. *Do I look as though I'm joking?*' His eyes blazed in his handsome face and she took an involuntary step backwards, startled by the violence of his response.

Clearly he wasn't joking. And if she needed confirmation of the degree of stress that he was under, then she had it now. It was so unlike Rico to reveal anything of his feelings, to display the slightest loss of control, that for a moment she couldn't respond.

'It's just that I find it hard to believe she asked for me—'

His outraged reaction to her mumbled statement was instantaneous. 'I thought we agreed that we are *not* raking over old wounds here,' he bit out harshly, pacing across the room and narrowly avoiding knocking his head on a beam. He lifted a hand to the offending beam and for a moment she thought he was going to try and rip it out of the ceiling with his bare hands. Instead he glanced upwards with a look of incredulity, as if he couldn't quite believe that anyone could have designed a house like this one. 'This cottage is a death trap.'

'It probably wasn't designed for someone of your build,' she muttered, wishing that he'd just leave. He dominated her small sitting room with the width of his shoulders and the force of his powerful personality and everything she'd spent months trying to forget came flying back into her mind.

Like the way it felt to kiss the bronzed skin at the base of his throat. And the fact that if she did that he'd instantly retaliate by sliding a hand down her spine and taking her mouth. And Rico had turned kissing into an art form.

Memories crowded her mind and suddenly she needed him to leave with almost fevered desperation. Before she forgot that this was the man who had broken her dreams into tiny pieces. *Before she forgot that she felt absolutely nothing for him any more.*

But he showed no sign of leaving. Instead he stood with his legs planted firmly apart, determined to defy the beams and her ill-concealed hostility. 'Since her accident two weeks ago she has emerged from an unconscious state only once and your name was the only word she uttered. *Your name*.' That fact clearly offended him and he made no attempt whatsoever to hide his contempt and distaste for the situation in which he now found himself. 'And, whatever you may think to the contrary, Chiara was very fond of you.'

Stasia stared at him in fascinated silence, wondering how a man so ferociously intelligent could be so blind when it came to his family.

She might have told him that Chiara was anything but fond of her. She might have repeated the many painful conversations she'd had with his sister when he'd been locked away running his fantastically successful global business empire leaving her to the mercies of his family.

Chiara *hated* her.

The teenager had resented her almost from the moment Rico had married her and she'd played a large part in the final destruction of their doomed marriage.

But Rico adored his sister. And Stasia had decided that it wasn't her place to tell him the truth; that she didn't want to be responsible for creating a rift in that famed Sicilian institution: 'the family.'

Deep in thought, she contemplated what could possibly have driven Chiara to ask for her. She knew nothing about the workings of the unconscious mind.

Guilt?

A subconscious desire to apologize? A sudden realization that she'd been in the wrong?

There was a discreet cough from the doorway and Rico turned impatiently, visibly irritated by the intrusion.

'Enzo is on the phone, sir.' The bodyguard looked apologetic. 'The plane is ready for take-off.'

Rico sucked in a breath and turned back to her, his body language purposeful and impatient. 'We need to go now. I have to be back at the hospital. Already I have wasted too much time coming here in person.'

A fact he clearly regretted. He had the look of a man who would rather be anywhere else but standing in this cramped front room with a woman he despised, and Stasia was in no doubt whatsoever that had he believed that someone else could have persuaded her to board his plane then he would have immediately delegated the task. But he'd known that she would try and refuse. And he'd been forced to deal with the situation himself.

He really expected her to go with him.

After everything that had happened, he really expected her to go with him.

Suddenly she regretted not answering the phone. At least then she would have had some warning of his impending arrival. She would have been able to prepare herself mentally for the shock and pain of seeing him again.

If she'd known what was coming she could have gone into hiding.

Or would she?

If Chiara was truly asking for her—if she was as badly injured as Rico was implying—how could she refuse to go?

How could she deny the girl the opportunity to apologize if that was what she needed?

She licked dry lips, knowing that she would never be able to live with herself if something happened to Chiara and she had refused to visit. The girl had been unbelievably cruel but Stasia was more than ready to forgive her. She'd always hoped that one day Chiara would find the courage to tell the truth.

But how could she go back there? *Back to where it had all happened.* And to face his family, who hated her so much, who'd thought she was so unsuitable for Rico.

She closed her eyes briefly and accepted the inevitable. Facing the enemy seemed less daunting than facing her own conscience should the unthinkable happen to the injured girl and she'd failed to visit. 'Give me five minutes to pack a bag.'

Rico let out a breath and some of the tension left his broad shoulders and it was only then that she realized that he'd been expecting to fight a battle. She suppressed a cynical smile. He obviously didn't realize that her taste for battles was long gone.

'You don't need to pack. You took nothing when you left.'

'I left everything because there was nothing I needed.' She met his gaze full on, the message clear in her eyes. *I was never interested in your money and I can't believe you don't know that.*

The only thing she'd ever needed was *him*, she thought sadly, and that had been the one thing he'd failed to understand. Clearly accustomed to women who craved access to his bottomless bank account, he'd been totally bemused by her indifference to his staggering wealth.

For a man driven by money and power, something as simple as love was as difficult to understand as a foreign language. And the more jewels and extravagant presents he'd given her, the less she'd felt like a wife and the more she'd felt like a mistress. It had been as if he was *paying* her for sex.

Reminding herself that all that was in the past, she

glanced down at her paint-stained jeans. 'At least let me change.'

She was past caring what his family thought of her but even she drew the line at entering a hospital covered in more paint than her easel.

'You can change on the plane,' he stated immediately, already striding towards her door, very much in control as usual. A man used to commanding those around him.

And she was going along with it. *But only for Chiara.*

She shook her head, exasperated with herself. She was independent in every sense of the word. And yet when Rico snapped his fingers she jumped. Every time. *And usually into his bed.*

But not this time.

Never again.

She closed her eyes briefly, suddenly overwhelmed by the enormity of what she was about to do. Did an alcoholic take a job in a brewery? Did a drug addict surround himself with illegal substances? And yet here she was about to walk off with the one man who made her forget the very person she was.

She must be mad.

Mad to put herself through the torture of being close to Rico for a teenage girl who had never shown her the slightest degree of warmth or friendship.

Aware that Rico was still watching her, impatience stamped all over his handsome features, she walked towards the door, her palms suddenly clammy and her heart thudding uncomfortably in her chest.

'All right. But this is going to be a short visit,' she muttered, her green eyes fixed on his, not allowing him to evade the issue. 'I see Chiara, I talk to her, I leave.

And you have your fancy plane waiting to bring me home.'

In normal circumstances she would have preferred to walk barefoot from Italy than avail herself of one of the trappings of his incredible wealth but these were not normal circumstances and she wanted to spend as little time as possible in the company of his family.

His lips curled. 'You can rest assured that I have no intention of prolonging your visit any longer than necessary.'

Of course he hadn't. Anger and misery mingled inside her. This had to be as difficult for him as it was for her. He'd made no secret of the fact that he'd made an enormous mistake in marrying her. That she wasn't the type of woman he wanted to have a permanent place by his side. *Just in his bed. Or any other available flat surface.*

She tried to ignore the intense shaft of pain that stabbed through her body, and reached for her keys and her bag. For a brief moment her eyes flickered to those wide shoulders, displayed in all their glory by the fabric of his perfectly cut designer suit. He had a fantastic body and from the first glimpse she'd been addicted. Dressed, the man was spectacular enough, but *undressed*—

The sudden memory of sleek, bronzed skin, of powerful muscle and dark, masculine body hair exploded into her brain and she shook her head slightly, trying to free herself from the seductive image imprinted on her mind.

As if sensing her sudden shift in thought pattern, he turned and their eyes locked with a fierce, mutual awareness that simply intensified the images in her brain.

Fire and flame surged between them and she felt herself take a step towards him in an instinctive response to the wild attraction that still existed.

For a brief moment something burned in his dark eyes and then it was extinguished and all that was left was ice.

She stopped dead, rendered immobile by the contempt she read in that cold gaze, remembering too late the two lessons that her marriage to Rico Crisanti had taught her.

That attraction, however powerful, was a shaky and precarious basis for a relationship.

And that loving someone with every beat of her heart didn't mean happy ever after.

CHAPTER TWO

'FEEL free to use the bathroom. You know where it is.' Rico was sprawled on the cream leather seat, his laptop computer open next to him, papers covered in figures spread across the desk. As usual, his ear had been stuck to the phone since the moment they'd become airborne and he'd barely glanced in her direction since she'd sat down and fastened her seat belt.

Nothing changed.

Stasia closed her eyes, flayed by his indifference and furious with herself for caring. She didn't care. She really didn't. It was just the shock of seeing him.

And of course she knew where the bathroom was. It was next to the bedroom. The same bedroom where he'd once carried her, laughing and crazily in love with him. *The same bedroom where he'd once made love to her for an entire flight.*

Her eyes opened and her gaze settled on the door at the back of his sumptuous private jet.

She'd spent twelve painful months trying to put it all behind her. Trying to free herself of the agonizing wanting and needing that tore into her at unexpected moments. Was walking through that door going to undo the little progress she'd made?

Oh, hell. It was just a bedroom, she reasoned, rising to her feet in a determined movement and pacing to the back of the plane, feeling the thick cream carpet give under her feet. And anyway, she didn't have to go near the bedroom. She'd just wash off the paint and make herself decent enough to face his disapproving, dependent family.

Rico was talking on the phone again and her hand stilled on the handle of the bedroom suite as she listened.

When she'd first met him she'd loved to hear him speaking Italian.

It didn't matter what he was saying. He could have been reading the financial pages of a newspaper and still the sound of his voice would have made her stomach turn over and her body tremble. He'd teased her about it but she hadn't cared.

Rico speaking Italian was verbal seduction.

Not wanting to relive those early days of their relationship, days that had been dominated by the most unbelievable sexual excitement, she opened the door to the bedroom suite and locked herself in the stylish bathroom.

She didn't want to think about the beginning of their relationship.

The only way she was going to survive the next few days was to remember the reasons why it had ended.

She stared in the mirror, noticed the splodge of paint above her right eyebrow and gave a wry smile.

She looked nothing like the wife of one of the world's most successful businessmen.

Which was probably why they were currently in the throes of a divorce, she thought numbly, turning on the taps and splashing her face with cool water in an attempt to remove the paint and tone down the colour in her flushed cheeks.

She was completely wrong for him.

But wasn't that what had first attracted Rico to her?

The fact that she was different from his usual diet of models and actresses?

He'd been attracted to her because she was different, but ultimately it had been those very differences that had driven them apart.

Reaching for a towel, she dried her face and studied her reflection. What had Rico seen in her, that day in Rome? What was it about her that had driven him to approach her? Despite her resolve not to think about it, her mind wandered.

She'd been balanced on scaffolding, working on the mural she'd been commissioned to paint on one wall of the foyer. As usual when she drew or painted, she'd been totally absorbed in her art and it was only after she'd completed the intricate task she'd set herself that she'd suddenly been aware that she was under scrutiny.

She glanced down and almost lost her balance.

In a country that appeared to be populated by gorgeous men, he was the most staggeringly sexy man she'd ever seen. Unmistakably Italian, breathtakingly good-looking and staring at *her*, those scorching dark eyes raking every inch of her with blatant male appreciation.

'Is everything OK?' Her Italian was embarrassingly bad so she used English, hoping that he would understand her.

Since she'd started painting the mural on one wall of the foyer of the international headquarters of the Crisanti Corporation, a steady stream of people had stopped and watched her but she'd never felt remotely uncomfortable. In fact she'd hardly noticed them. But no woman could fail to notice this man. He was unreasonably handsome and she had to stop herself from drooling as her artist's eye roved over his perfect bone structure and the strong, symmetrical planes of his face. Her fingers twitched and if she'd had a pencil handy she would have sketched him instantly. Which would have been a frustrating exercise, she acknowledged dreamily. No two-dimensional drawing would ever be able to reflect the strength and power of the man in front of her.

He stood like a god, confident and all-powerful, and there was something about his cool, steady gaze that made her uncharacteristically nervous.

Noticing that the foyer seemed unusually full of people for the time of day, she glanced at his companions, noted their build and the respectful distance they kept, and finally realized just exactly who was scrutinizing her so closely.

She hastily descended the ladder and wiped the palm of her hand down her jeans before extending it. 'I'm Anastasia Silver. I'm a commercial artist. I was awarded the contract for painting your mural.'

Your mural—

She cringed as she heard herself speak. As if someone in Rico Crisanti's position was going to know or care who was decorating his office building. He undoubtedly left decisions like that to lesser mortals and concentrated his legendary brain power on amassing further millions to add to his already staggering fortune.

His hand closed over hers and she almost gasped at the strength and power of that grip. Aware that his gaze had shifted to the wall that she'd been painting, she followed his gaze, suddenly seeing it through his eyes and feeling a lurch of horror. Ideally she liked to work on a project in private until it was completed, but in this case it hadn't been possible.

'You're probably thinking that it looks terrible but it

always does at this stage. It's hard to imagine what it will look like when it's finished. In many ways the preparation is as important as the final painting. I—your architect approved my drawings and colour sketches,' she tailed off lamely, aware that his attention was now fixed firmly on her face.

'Are you always this tense? If so then I'm amazed you can wield a brush,' he murmured, bestowing her with an unexpected smile. 'Relax, Miss Silver. I like what you're doing to my wall.'

His wall.

He made it sound intimate. Personal. As if the wall was part of him.

Flayed by the seductive charm of that smile, Stasia felt her knees wobble and the colour rise in her cheeks.

Utterly self-conscious and not liking the feeling one little bit, she bit her lip and took a few steps backwards, suddenly realizing what a mess she must look.

'I'm covered in paint.' She lifted a hand to her burning cheeks, just hating herself for being so gauche when she should have been cool. 'I must look a total mess.'

His smile was the smile of a male well aware that if a woman was worrying about her appearance then he was home and dry.

'*Not* a mess. And I love your hair,' he assured her smoothly, registering her extreme discomfort with no small degree of amusement. 'So many shades of gold and copper blended together. It reminds me of England in the autumn.' His dark eyes scanned her hair in minute detail as if he were determined to memorize every strand. 'Apart from the white spotted bits.'

Feeling a deadly warmth spread through her body, Stasia fingered her wild curls. 'It will wash out.'

One dark eyebrow swooped upwards. 'The autumn gold? I hope not.'

'The white spots,' she muttered, glancing around her and wondering what the rest of his entourage was making of this ridiculous conversation. 'The first thing I do in the evening is get rid of the paint.'

He nodded, his gaze suddenly thoughtful. 'I should very much like to see you without the paint, Miss Silver. You will have dinner with me tonight.'

His arrogant assurance that she'd say yes outraged her intellect but her body was already trembling with anticipation. 'I might be busy.'

He smiled. The smile of a man totally confident in his own appeal. 'Eight o'clock. And you won't be busy.'

Still unable to believe that Rico Crisanti had asked her out, Stasia had to remind herself to breathe. 'Sure of yourself, aren't you?' She lifted an eyebrow in mockery. 'Is that a legacy from your Roman ancestors? Do you have the same fundamental need to conquer, pillage and plunder, I wonder?'

'That depends on the prize.' Dark eyes rested on her mouth with masculine fascination. 'And I'm not Roman, Miss Silver. I'm Sicilian. And we have a very different way of doing things.'

Without waiting for her to reply, he finally lifted his gaze from her mouth and strolled across the foyer towards the lift, followed at a respectful distance by his minions.

Stasia stared after him, stunned into a silence driven by disbelief. Not Roman. *Sicilian.*

Rico Crisanti, one of the richest and most powerful men in the world, wanted to have dinner with her.

For a wild, impulsive moment her heart leaped and her imagination followed.

And then reality interceded.

What would a man like Rico Crisanti want with her?

Compared to his usual diet of sleek, rich women she was a mongrel.

Her slim shoulders tensed and her mouth fell open at his arrogance. He'd just *assumed* that she'd want to spend an evening with him.

But then what woman would ever say no to him?

Confronted by temptation in its purest form, Stasia reminded herself that he hadn't even asked where she was staying so it was highly unlikely that he'd turn up at eight. And if he did—

She climbed back up the scaffolding and tried to continue with the design on the wall, ignoring the fact that her concentration was broken and her hand wasn't quite steady.

If he did, then she'd just have to tell him that she didn't have dinner with strangers.

Dragging her mind back to the present, Stasia showered and quickly plaited her heavy mane of copper hair so that it fell in a neat tube between her narrow shoulder blades.

Then she turned her attention to the wardrobe.

There were numerous designer outfits, all quite formal and not to her taste but towards the back of the rail she found a simple linen dress in a soft shade of peach. Simple in all but cost, she thought wryly as she caught a glimpse of the label. It was miles away from her usually colourful, casual style but it was that or paint-spattered jeans so she slipped it on anyway. One critical glance in the mirror told her that it suited her.

She looked elegant and classy.

Like a fortune hunter?

She bit her lip and then dismissed the thought. It was too late to start worrying again about what his family thought of her. Far too late.

She left the luxurious bathroom, chin held high, and settled herself back in the cream leather seat.

Rico was still on the phone and she gritted her teeth, remembering how many times she'd threatened to throw his phone away when they'd been together. She stared blankly out of the window, feeling steadily sicker as she contemplated the meeting ahead of her.

She actually hadn't seen Chiara since that fatal evening a year previously—

It was a moment or two before she realized that Rico had finally stopped talking and had transferred his lean, muscular length to the seat next to her.

'I'm sorry to just abandon you like that,' he said in cool tones, stretching out a hand for the drink that the uniformed hostess had prepared for him. 'There were calls I needed to make. That dress suits you.'

The unexpected compliment startled her and when his broad shoulder brushed against hers she had to stop herself from jumping back in her seat. She felt the tension spread through her body, felt the exaggerated beat of her heart against her chest as her body responded to his nearness. She breathed in his tantalizing male scent and suddenly all her senses throbbed and hummed. He was her power source. One touch and her entire body sizzled with sexual energy.

Angry with herself, she shifted in her seat.

What was the matter with her?

How could she still want him, knowing what sort of

man he was? Knowing that he didn't want her anywhere other than the bedroom?

Not once in their relationship had he actually said he loved her. So how had she managed to fool herself, even for a short time, that he might?

Because of the way he held her and touched her, she acknowledged miserably. For a short, blissful time she'd confused the touch of a man in love with that of a man who was a skilled lover. *Not* the same thing, as she'd eventually discovered to her cost.

Discreetly moving so that their arms were no longer touching, she glanced at him, attempting to match the indifference he was displaying. 'We both know this isn't a social visit,' she replied, her tone every bit as cool as his. 'I don't expect to be entertained and I certainly don't expect to interrupt your business. I never did when we were married. I finally accepted that you were, in fact, already married to your mobile phone. Why would I expect anything different now?'

For Rico, business came first.

'Don't bait me, Stasia.' He shot her a cold look. 'I'm not in the mood and since we can no longer end our rows in bed there seems little point in having them.'

The mere mention of bed made her tummy tumble and, against her will, her eyes dropped to his beautifully sculpted mouth. He'd kissed her into silence on more occasions than she cared to remember. When they'd both been devoured by the flames of anger it had been sex which had quenched that anger and left them both spent.

It was the only level on which they had communicated. Only even then they'd been saying different things. She'd been saying *I love you* while he'd been saying *I want you.*

Her eyes lifted to his. 'I'm not baiting you.'

'Yes, you are. With every flash of your green eyes and every word you don't speak.' His eyes narrowed and something shifted in his dark gaze. 'And it wasn't business. For your information, my first call was to a neurosurgeon who specializes in traumatic brain injury. I wanted to seek his opinion on the possibility of brain damage and make sure that there are no procedures that have been overlooked that could help Chiara. My second call was to the friend who she was staying with at the time of the accident and the third was to the hospital in Sicily. Having now been away from her side for most of the day, naturally I was keen for an update.'

'Sicily?' She stared at him, aghast, diverted from uncomfortable thoughts by the sheer shock of hearing his last statement. 'We're going to *Sicily*?'

He frowned. '*Si*, where did you think?'

'Rome.' She lifted a hand to her throat, feeling her pulse beating rapidly under her fingers. 'I assumed we were going to Rome.'

He had offices all over the globe but the headquarters of the Crisanti Corporation were in Rome. It was where he spent a large proportion of his time.

He shrugged dismissively, as if her misunderstanding were of no consequence. 'You assumed wrongly. Chiara was in Sicily at the time of her accident. That is where we are going.'

Back to the birthplace of her dreams. Back to the scene of perfect happiness. It would be the cruellest taunt he could have devised and for a moment she wondered whether he'd planned it. Did he hate her so much that he'd knowingly cause her that much pain?

'I don't want to go to Sicily!' The words left her mouth before she could prevent them and she closed her eyes, cursing her own lack of control and that impetuous streak in her nature that always caused her to reveal too much. If he'd intended to hurt her then she'd just given him the satisfaction of knowing he'd succeeded.

'Why? Why don't you want to go to Sicily?' His tone was harsh and if he was feeling smug then he was certainly displaying no outward signs of the fact. 'Conscience pricking you, Stasia? Remembering the beginning of our relationship? All those things you said and didn't mean? All those empty words of love?'

Empty?

She turned her head away from him, wondering how a man of his intelligence could be so blind.

The weeks they'd spent together in Sicily on their honeymoon had been the happiest time of their relationship and she'd trusted Rico completely. Had opened her heart without holding back. Had given everything.

Only now could she see how foolish she'd been.

How naïve and trusting.

Rico had never wanted what she'd wanted. Hadn't been capable of giving what she'd wanted him to give.

'Perhaps I should have kept you trapped on Sicily,' he said acidly. 'That way you wouldn't have had the opportunity to pursue your seemingly endless desire for variety.'

With a gasp of pain she turned towards him, her eyes flashing with contempt. 'I was *never* unfaithful to you.'

He flared up with such speed that she recoiled with shock. 'I find you with a naked man in your room and you expect me to believe that it was innocent?' He leaned towards her, his voice a primitive male growl, streaks of colour highlighting the arresting angle of his cheekbones. 'You were my *wife*. And you didn't even hang around to defend yourself. What does that make you, if not guilty?'

Anger smothered her ability to breathe normally. 'I saw the look in your eyes, Rico. You were beyond rational conversation. But you should have known me well enough to know that I would *never* have betrayed you. You should not have believed it of me, Rico!'

He turned on her like a beast in pain. '*Dio*, I saw him kiss you. *You were mine and I saw him kiss you.*'

One glance and he'd assumed he had all the facts. He was so primitive and possessive that it hadn't occurred to him that there might be another explanation for the scene in front of him.

At the time she'd been so shocked and appalled herself that she'd found herself without the means for defence. And part of her had felt that the innocent shouldn't need defence. She'd waited and waited for Chiara to tell the truth but the teenager had just given a small smile and slipped back to her room, leaving Stasia with an impossible decision to make.

Did she tell him the truth about his sister?

Confused, hurt and angry, in the end she'd just left, deciding that they both needed time to calm down. She'd walked out in the middle of the night, taking nothing with her but her passport.

But, instead of seeing her departure as a cooling off period, he'd seen her exit as further confirmation of her guilt.

And when she'd cooled down enough to swallow her pride and call him, he'd blocked her calls.

And that had been that. In one bleak moment she'd been damned.

He hadn't been able to believe in her and she hadn't been able to forgive him for that; she had known she couldn't live with a man like him. It had been the final straw in a marriage that had already been under strain. The next communication she'd had with him had been through his lawyers.

Stasia reached for the seat belt, her hands shaking as she fumbled with the buckle.

He frowned sharply as he watched her. 'What the hell are you doing?'

'Getting away from you. I was wrong to come. I can't see how my presence can possibly help Chiara. I'm sure that the last thing she needs is tension and that's all she'll get if you and I are by her bed together.'

'You're not going anywhere.' Long, strong fingers closed over hers, preventing her attempts to free herself. 'We are landing shortly. Keep the belt *on*.'

'I want to go home. And until I can go home I intend to stay in the bathroom. I don't want to breathe the same air as you.' She tried to free her hands from his but he held her easily, his strength so much greater than hers that it was laughable.

'*Dio*, sit *still*!'

'I want you to tell your pilot to turn this fancy toy of yours round and fly me home.' She still struggled but without any conviction that she could free herself. 'I'm not going *anywhere* with you.'

'You've already agreed to go to the hospital,' he reminded her curtly and she rounded on him, hurt and pain making her voice shake.

She hated him so much. She really, really hated him for being so cold and unfeeling. For not believing in her. *For not loving her.*

'To visit your sister, yes, but *not* to be insulted by you. I never agreed to that. I've been attacked enough by your family.'

He drew in a breath sharply and she knew from the dangerous flash of his eyes that he was struggling with his temper. That temper which he prided himself on having totally under control. *Except with her.* With her he shot fire and flame. No holding back. It was like watching a long dormant volcano suddenly come to life in a terrifying eruption. But his temper had never frightened her. In fact for some strange reason it had comforted her to know that Rico was capable of displaying emotion, even if it was anger. At least *something* threatened his cool.

'To deal with your first point—obviously we are going to Sicily, since that is where Chiara is.' He looked at her with ill-disguised impatience. 'Despite your worst assessment of my character I do, in fact, care about my family.'

Stasia froze. It was his obsession with family, so much a part of his Sicilian heritage, that had blinded him to the truth. And it had been that same deep love for his family that had prevented her from telling him the truth about his sister. How could she shatter his illusions?

'I've never doubted your love for your family,' she muttered, wondering why on earth they were discussing all this now, when it was all much, much too late. 'You said that you rang the hospital. Has there been any change?'

His glance was as contemptuous as it was chilly. 'Why ask, when we both know that you don't really care?'

Stasia gave a soft gasp of shock. She cared. Just as she'd cared when it had first become apparent that his family thought he'd made a mistake in marrying her. The first few barbed comments about her supposed obsession with his money had upset her badly. And those same comments had taken away any pleasure that she might have felt when Rico had showered her with gifts. In the end she'd stopped wearing the jewels that he was continually giving her, unable to cope with the knowing looks of his mother and sister. In case, by wearing them, she gave some credence to their unsavoury assumptions about her.

'I care, Rico.' Suddenly it seemed important to say it. To set the record straight on that, at least. 'If you truly believe that then it shows how little you know me,' she said stiffly and those glittering dark eyes clashed with hers.

'I established how little I know you some time ago,' he said, his voice cold and unforgiving. 'But, unfortunately for me, not before I'd married you. Had I known your true nature I never would have invited you into my home. And you would never have had the opportunity to corrupt my sister. You took her to nightclubs when you knew I had expressly forbidden her to frequent those places and goodness knows what else you encouraged.'

Stasia froze.

His accusation was so unjust—so far from the real truth of the situation—that for a moment she just stared at him.

How could he have been so intimate with her and still believe—?

'You're so wrong, Rico.' She'd promised herself that she wasn't going to waste any more energy in trying to defend herself but her sense of fair play was so strong that she couldn't stay silent. 'And one day you are going to go down on one knee and beg my forgiveness.'

'Save it,' he said harshly, his darkened jaw set at an

aggressive angle. 'You were caught out, my beautiful wife. Admit that you were in the wrong and perhaps we can move on.'

Move on?

Where to?

Hot tears suddenly pricked her eyes and she turned her head towards the window, desperate to compose herself before he noticed her distress. She refused to give him the satisfaction of knowing that he'd upset her.

And she was honest enough to acknowledge that the demise of their relationship couldn't be blamed entirely on the manipulative ways of his sister. Had they truly been a couple—*had there been more to their relationship than sex*—then he never would have believed those things of her. Never would have believed her capable of the things of which she was accused. Forced to acknowledge that their relationship had been doomed from the beginning, she sank back into her seat and he immediately released her hands.

'We will be landing in ten minutes,' he informed her curtly, 'and we'll go straight to the hospital.'

Stasia took a deep breath, telling herself that there was no benefit in raking up the past. She just needed to get through the present—this visit—and then she could go home. Away from him. To try and calm herself, she kept the conversation in the present.

'How did the accident happen?'

'She was staying on a friend's estate.' Rico rested his head against the seat and closed his eyes, as if doing so made it easier to recount the awful details. 'They went riding. Something frightened her horse and it bolted on to the road. Chiara came off and she wasn't wearing a hat.'

Stasia winced as a mental vision of the accident filled

her mind and for a moment she stared at him, at the thick dark lashes touching his bronzed skin, at the firm mouth and the perfect lines of his face. With his eyes closed he seemed less the ruthless businessman and more human. Less intimidating and more vulnerable.

More the man she'd fallen in love with.

As if feeling her gaze, he opened his eyes and Stasia looked away quickly, reminding herself that there was nothing vulnerable about Rico Crisanti.

He was everything tough.

She turned back to him, needing to speak. Needing to say something. Unlike him, she couldn't keep her emotions locked away. 'Whatever happened between us, I want you to know that I'm sorry about Chiara. Truly I am. This must all be so hard for you. The not knowing, the waiting—' She glanced at him cautiously and for a moment she thought she saw a wry smile touch his mouth.

'*Not* my strong point, as you well know,' he drawled, glancing at his watch as the plane taxied to a halt. 'We've arrived. I should warn you that my entire family presently inhabits the hospital. Tensions are running high and the atmosphere is already more emotional than is desirable. Needless to say your arrival is hardly going to be greeted with enthusiasm.'

The reminder that his family hated her was like a cold shower, quenching her tentative attempt to build bridges.

'You asked me to come,' she reminded him stiffly and he gave a sigh and stabbed long fingers through his sleek, glossy hair.

'*Si*, I was given no choice in the matter. Chiara asked for you. That was enough for me.' Stormy black eyes clashed with hers in blatant warning. 'But not all my family share my opinion. I would ask you to keep your outspoken views to yourself on this occasion.'

In other words she wasn't allowed to step out of line. And suddenly she realized just how hard this must be for him. Not just because of Chiara, but because of *her*. He'd cut her out of his life. To him she'd ceased to exist except as a name on various legal papers. And now circumstances had forced him to invite her back into his life. And he clearly *hated* that fact.

'Your family may not approve of me but that is their problem, not mine,' she said with quiet dignity. 'You've asked me to come here. You can't expect me to change my personality as well.'

He swore fluently. 'I am not asking you to change your personality! Just to show some sensitivity to the situation. They are understandably stressed by Chiara's condition. They do not need further pressure.'

This was not going to be a happy meeting. And, with that grim thought, she unfastened her seat belt and followed him to the front of the plane.

CHAPTER THREE

THEY drove from the airport to the hospital without exchanging another word.

Again Rico was attached to his mobile phone, his lean hands moving in silent emphasis as he spoke in rapid Italian. In the front, his driver and a bodyguard sat in watchful silence.

Stasia knew without looking that another car with bodyguards would be travelling immediately behind them. Rico's high profile status as a billionaire tycoon made such precautions mandatory and she'd grown accustomed to having company during their whirlwind courtship and the six months of their marriage. She'd even had fun behaving outrageously, knowing that they were being watched almost all the time.

To Stasia's surprise, they avoided the entrance of the huge modern hospital and instead Rico's driver steered the car down a series of side streets before pulling up outside an alleyway. There was a fire escape at the end and at the top of the fire escape, a door.

'Why are we going this way?'

'Because all the conventional entrances to the hospital are teeming with paparazzi,' Rico explained, his handsome face grim as he led her quickly down the narrow passage. 'This route leads into a corridor near the intensive care unit. So far the press don't seem to have discovered it.'

Safely inside the hospital, he strode purposefully along the corridor and paused outside the unit, anxiety stamped on every line of his bronzed features.

'Wait here.'

Stasia stood outside the entrance to the intensive care unit, her heart thudding against her chest. The prospect of meeting his family again made her gasp for air and when he reappeared by her side and announced that he was taking her straight to Chiara, she felt a flicker of relief that the inevitable confrontation with his family would be postponed.

The teenage girl lay still, her face as pale as the hospital sheets that covered her. A bruise cast a bluish haze over one side of her face and, next to her, frighteningly high-tech machines bleeped and hummed as they monitored every aspect of her condition. Confronted by the brutal evidence of medical technology, Stasia felt a sickness build in her stomach. Rico's brief, almost sparse, description of his sister's injuries hadn't prepared her for the horrifying reality of seeing someone so seriously injured.

Suddenly she realized just how strong he really was. He was living in a nightmare and yet he was still managing to function. To run a company, to prop up his family, to come and fetch her even though it must be the last thing he wanted—

She felt hot tears prick her eyes. Even now, he was only able to show his emotions in peripheral ways. He looked tired. He looked tense. But he still couldn't talk about how he felt. And that had been one of the fundamental differences between them.

How many times during their all too brief relationship had she wished he would really *talk* to her?

How many times had she waited to hear him say that he loved her?

But he'd never spoken those words.

And she knew now that it was because he never had

loved her. For a while he'd wanted her but not any more. Now he despised her.

The bleak reality of the situation swamped her. The tears spilled over and her legs started to shake. She didn't think she'd made a sound but she must have done because she heard him mutter something and the next moment he was by her side, a strong hand on her shoulder, a frown bringing his dark brows together.

'You are incredibly pale. Are you feeling unwell? It is very hot in here and the atmosphere is oppressive. I should have warned you.'

She struggled with the tears, wondering how there could still be tears left inside her. Surely during the past year she'd cried herself out? Mourning the death of their relationship, of her dreams. Missing him so much that the pain was almost a physical torment.

She really, *really* shouldn't be thinking about this now but there was something about the sterile, cold atmosphere of the hospital that made her feel more isolated and alone than ever before. *More aware of just how fleeting and fragile life really was.*

She felt the taste of salt on her lips and brushed away the tears with the back of her hand. 'I'm sorry—'

'Don't be.' His voice was rough and loaded with self-recrimination. 'Hospitals are not nice places at the best of times and in these circumstances—' He broke off and pushed her gently towards the nearest chair.

She sank on to it gratefully and looked helplessly at Chiara. The girl lay still, oblivious to anything going on around her.

Rico gave a driven sigh and took the chair next to her. 'Our lives do not always turn out the way we expect, do they?' His gruff tone betrayed a depth of emotion that she'd given up ever hearing him express and the strain was etched in his own dark features as he lifted his sister's limp hand.

For a moment he was silent, as if rallying himself, and then he sucked in a breath and fastened his gaze on his sister's face. 'Stasia is here—' The control was back, the emotion gone, and for a moment she wondered whether she'd imagined it. More comfortable in his own language, he switched to Italian, talking swiftly and gently, all the time holding Chiara's hand as if hoping to transfer some of his vital strength to the injured girl.

Stasia sat in frozen stillness, the tears now blocked somewhere deep inside her, staring at the girl who had made no secret of hating her. It was almost impossible to believe that she was the same person.

In her unconscious state, Chiara had lost all her defiance.

Instead she looked like a very young, very vulnerable teenager and Stasia felt her resentment melt away.

Rico lifted his head and looked at her, the strain making his eyes seem even darker than usual. 'The doctors thought it might help if she were to hear your voice— if you could say something. Talk to her.'

Stasia looked at him helplessly. This was *so* hard. She wanted to help, but what on earth was she supposed to talk about? The past? Hardly—when almost all their conversations had been hostile. Certainly on Chiara's part. Almost since the day Stasia had married Rico, Chiara had treated her as the enemy.

Aware that Rico was watching her expectantly, Stasia leaned closer to the bed, feeling more self-conscious than she ever had in her life before. If she said the wrong thing now—

'Hi, Chiara—' She broke off and cleared her throat. 'It's Stasia.'

She paused for a moment, half-expecting Chiara to leap from her bed and slap her around the face.

But the girl didn't move. Didn't respond in any way.

Suddenly she wished Rico would go for a walk. Leave them alone. But there was no chance of that, of course. He thought she was a corrupting influence and there was no way he'd leave her alone with his much younger sister. 'What have you done to yourself? Why weren't you wearing a hat? Maybe some gorgeous boy was watching and you didn't want to hide your hair—'

She caught Rico's sharp frown but ignored him. If she was going to talk to Chiara then she was going to talk about things that might make sense to the girl. Something that reflected the person she was. It would have been typical of Chiara to ignore the hat if someone was watching.

Stasia hesitated for a moment and then gently touched Chiara's shoulder.

'Everyone's pretty worried about you. Your brother's even taken a day off work—that should tell you how bad it is. Can't remember him ever taking a day off before now, can you? So if you don't want the Crisanti Corporation to collapse then you'd better start thinking about waking up—' She continued to talk, keeping it lighthearted, chatting about everything and nothing until finally Rico stood up in a sudden movement, almost as if he couldn't stand it any longer.

'That's enough for now.' His voice was rough and he seemed almost unbearably tense as he raked long fingers through his hair. 'It's getting late. You need some rest.'

'I'd rather stay.' She didn't want to leave the injured girl's bedside if there was a chance her presence could make a difference.

'You look worn out.' The words were dragged from

him, as if he was afraid she might misinterpret his concern as something sweeter.

But there was no chance of that. She knew exactly what he thought of her and knew that the fact that she was here was a measure of his love for his sister. Not an indication of any feeling for her. He had none. Or at least, nothing positive and she was miserably aware that nothing but desperation on his part would have induced him to make contact with someone he held in such contempt.

The knowledge choked her. 'It's been a stressful day.' Her voice was strangely flat and suddenly she realized that he was right. She *was* exhausted. She'd been painting non stop, throwing herself into her work, trying to forget—

'You haven't changed.' His voice was heavily accented and suddenly he sounded very, very Sicilian. 'You're still obsessed with your work. Do you realize you talked about virtually nothing else?'

Because there was nothing else in her life to talk about.

She managed an ironic smile, because that was undoubtedly what he would have expected from her. 'And this coming from you?' Her tone was dry but he didn't return the smile.

'And you still talk too much.'

Stasia's own smile faded at that bittersweet reminder of their past. He'd always teased her about that. The fact that she chatted all the time. 'I thought you wanted me to talk.'

He paced to the end of the bed as if he needed to distance himself from something. 'I did. But it's enough for one night. Enough for both of you. Today has been difficult for all of us.' His eyes met hers, his dark gaze conveying just *how* difficult. 'I'll arrange for you to be taken home.'

Home?

She swallowed, wondering if he even realized what he'd said. 'Don't get cosy with me, Rico. This isn't my home any more. We both know that.'

And she didn't want to be here a moment longer than necessary. Being this close to him tore her apart, inside and out.

She wanted to hurl herself on his broad chest and claw at him until he begged forgiveness for throwing away what they'd shared without trying harder to protect it. *Until he explained why he hadn't come after her. Why he'd let her leave.*

For a fierce, stormy moment his eyes clashed with hers and then he muttered something in Italian and his hands curled into fists.

'For the final time, we are still married.'

If ever she needed a reminder that their views on that particular institution were vastly different, that was it.

'I want to go to a hotel.'

'No hotel.'

'Rico—'

'Until she wakes up I want you at the villa, so that I know where you are. After that—' he gave a dismissive shrug '—you are free to go.'

She struggled with the familiar frustration. As usual he dictated. There was no question of him even *considering* her opinion. He was used to commanding and being obeyed.

She tossed her head back, her hair tumbling like fire down her slender back. 'I can make my own decisions, Rico,' she informed him in a hoarse voice. 'I'm not one of your employees.'

'No. You're my wife.' His voice was cold. 'And you would do well to remember it.'

She gasped. 'This is not the time for your macho Sicilian possessive streak—' She broke off, silenced by the warning look from his glittering black eyes.

And suddenly she knew. Knew that he was feeling the same pressures that she was.

He still wanted her. And that knowledge must be killing him.

If she hadn't been so angry, so wrenched apart by misery, she would have smiled. After the accusations he'd flung at her, the things he'd been willing to believe about her, to still want her must offend his sensibilities. For a man who had to control everything, not being able to control his physical response to her must be galling in the extreme.

But she didn't feel like smiling. She felt like screaming, like sobbing, like hitting him.

The hopelessness of it all, *the waste*, just flayed her. It didn't have to be like this. It could have been so different.

'Rico—'

Immediately he withdrew from her, both physically and emotionally, his dark eyes shuttered, displaying the self-discipline that was so much a part of the man he was. 'If you have business obligations, then make calls,' he said coldly. 'Do what you have to do. But you will stay at the villa.'

She no longer had the energy to argue with him. Arguing with Rico required a set of fully charged batteries and at the moment hers were distinctly flat.

As if assuring himself that she no longer intended to fight, he stared at her face for endless moments and then gave an almost imperceptible nod. 'I'll have you driven to the villa.'

The villa where they'd spent so much time together. Where they'd been so happy. She couldn't really believe he intended her to stay there. Surely it would increase the torture for both of them?

Or maybe he just didn't care that much.

She straightened her shoulders. 'What about you? You need sleep, too.'

She didn't question why, after everything that had happened, she was worrying about him. Rico Crisanti wasn't a man who needed or wanted the sympathy of others. He preferred to be seen as invulnerable.

His gaze was shuttered, forbidding any access to his emotions. 'I have some calls to make. I prefer to stay at the hospital.'

Part of her withered and died as the implications of his harsh statement penetrated her sluggish brain.

So that was why he was sending her to the villa. He had no intention of being there himself. Of sharing any part of himself with her. The knowledge made her ache and she looked away, giving up all hope of connecting with him. He didn't want her concern. Didn't want to acknowledge his own emotions.

Why the hell had he sent her to the villa?

Four hours later Rico was slumped in an unbelievably uncomfortable chair in the relatives' room that he had come to hate over the past few weeks. He'd finally decided that the peace of his villa held more attraction than this waiting room filled with his well-meaning but exhausting relatives. There had been no change in Chiara's condition, his mother and grandmother were insisting on staying at the hospital and the press were still baying like wolves, desperate for a story.

So why, when it was the only place that offered any sort of sanctuary from the unremitting strain of his current situation, had he sent her to the villa? What madness had possessed him?

And why, when he despised her from the very depth of his being, couldn't he get her out of his mind? His thoughts should have been filled with nothing but his sister, but he couldn't stop thinking about the one woman who had almost destroyed his sanity.

He clenched his fists and, without questioning himself too closely, glanced at the security guard in the doorway and instructed him to arrange for the car to take him to the villa.

Slumped in the back of the car, eyes gritty from lack of sleep, he acknowledged that the reason he'd sent her to the villa was because he didn't trust her not to leave if she went to a hotel. It was quite obvious that she didn't want to be here and she'd already proved that she was more than happy to run when the going got tough. And the going had got extremely tough, thanks to her taste for boys barely out of their teens. Jealousy shot through him and he grimaced as the pain flared, bright and agonizing as ever. Perhaps she'd been right to run. At the time he'd wanted to wring her neck with his bare hands, so running away had actually been a wise move on her part, although it had merely confirmed her guilt as far as he was concerned.

He strode into the villa with every muscle of his powerful body tensed in readiness, prepared for battle, but there was no sign of Stasia and he assumed she was already asleep. She'd certainly looked pale and exhausted when he'd finally sent her away from the hospital. Was it the strain of seeing Chiara, he wondered grimly, or the strain of seeing him? Was her conscience finally troubling her?

Dismissing the staff, he poured himself a drink and gave a grim smile, acknowledging the weakness of man.

Even knowing her tricks, knowing what she was capable of, he still wanted her. He'd taught himself to hate her and yet he still wanted her with a primitive desperation that drove almost everything else from his mind. Which just went to prove that their relationship had nothing to do with the mind and everything to do with the body, he reflected, taking his drink on to the terrace and standing for a moment with his face towards the sea.

Like it or not, Stasia was in his blood. And divorcing her wasn't going to change that fact. So the sooner he learned to live with it, the better for both of them.

It was just a reaction to his current situation, he assured himself. Seeking physical release was a natural male response to stress and tension and the tension in his life at the moment was reaching snapping point.

His thoughts turned to his sister and his shoulders sagged and his expression grew bleak. The strain of keeping it together for the rest of the family was starting to tell and he stared at the large swimming pool that lay just beyond the terrace, wondering whether a different form of exercise might relieve some of the pressure.

Later, he decided, pacing back inside and settling himself down on one of the long white sofas positioned to give an undisturbed view of the pool and the sea beyond.

The doctors had promised to call if there was any change and in the meantime he had some important calls to make. He was only too aware that his staff were making valiant attempts not to hound him but equally aware that his complex business empire didn't run itself.

He finished his drink, poured another one and then put in a call to his Finance Director, who was currently troubleshooting at the New York office.

An hour later he ended the call and picked at the plate

of cold meats that the maid had discreetly placed in front of him at some point earlier.

He ate without noticing the food, his head buried in a pile of papers that his assistant had sent over from the office. Occasionally he paused to scribble a note in the margin or make another phone call and it was after midnight when he finally tossed the papers on to the table and leaned back with his eyes closed.

The idea of a swim grew steadily more appealing and he rose to his feet in a fluid movement, stripping off his clothes as he walked towards the pool. The water shone blue, illuminated by a row of tiny lights that ran the length of the pool and he dived naked into the cool water, surfaced and swam to the other side with a powerful front crawl. He powered through the water with steady, even strokes, the physical demands he placed on himself sufficient to momentarily drive the present from his mind.

He felt her before he saw her.

Felt her presence on the poolside.

Something in the atmosphere changed. Something so subtle that to anyone else it would have been undetectable.

But not to him.

Their hyper-awareness of each other had always been part of their amazing physical relationship. Even in a crowded room he'd been able to sense her presence and he knew it was the same for her.

He surfaced, cleared the water from his eyes with a sweep of his bronzed hand, and saw her standing on the edge of the pool watching him, as slender and fragile as a young deer, her stunning fiery hair trailing loose over a white silk shirt.

His shirt.

'Stealing my clothes, Stasia?' Without thinking, he

spoke in Italian and he saw her quick indrawn breath, saw the shiver of response.

'I wasn't expecting to stay.' She replied in Italian, her voice smoky and slightly hesitant because she'd never been that confident in his language. 'I didn't pack anything.'

And usually she slept naked. While they'd been together, he'd never allowed her to do anything else. Had never wanted anything to hide her incredible body.

He switched to English. 'You always stole my shirts.'

And, with her innate sense of style, she'd managed to turn them into a fashion statement. She had a flair for making the ordinary extraordinary. A scarf tied in a certain way. Colours that no one else would dare to put together. Her artist's eye for design was visible in everything she touched.

And then there was her hair. A sinfully sexy mass of fire and flame that reflected the tempestuous nature of the woman. *It was enough to make a man lose his mind.*

She gave a tiny, almost imperceptible, shrug. 'You have good taste in shirts. I didn't think you were coming home. I heard someone in the pool—' Her voice still had the husky quality of the half-awake and even in the cool water he felt his body throb in response to her sleepy tones. How often had he woken her in the night to claim her body yet again, how often had she laughed softly and teased him in just such a tone as that?

He lifted himself out of the pool in an easy movement, seeing her eyes darken in response to his nakedness. His own eyes slid down, catching the movement of her slender throat as she swallowed, reading the unmistakable hunger in her glance before she concealed it with one sweep of her long, curling eyelashes.

His response to her involuntary glance was instantaneous and he reached for a towel that one of his staff had thoughtfully placed on a lounger, cursing his inability to remain indifferent to this woman. It was as if his body was out of his control. Which it was, of course. From the moment they'd met, he'd been under her spell. Made vulnerable by man's original temptation. Woman. *Only in his case just the one woman.*

Stasia.

'I had calls to make.' He wrapped the towel firmly round his waist, depriving her of the view. Perhaps if she stopped looking he'd stop reacting. 'Work to do. I needed a break from the hospital.'

And most of all from his relatives, he reflected wearily. He wasn't going to admit that to her but it was clear that she knew what he was thinking.

He could tell by the look in her eyes. Those all knowing, all seeing green eyes that took hold of a man and made him burn with wanting.

The silence around them throbbed and crackled with a tension that only the two of them felt and suddenly he was grateful for the towel. At least it hid the laughably predictable workings of his body. For a brief moment he wished he'd done as she'd requested and sent her to a hotel. Anywhere, as long as it was away from him.

Seeing her like this, half naked in his shirt, *in his home*, suggested an intimacy that no longer existed between them.

He had to remind himself that she was no longer his. That he no longer held the right to feel the primitive and possessive thoughts that had such an iron grip on his normally logical brain.

It didn't help that she wanted him too. He could tell by the way her soft mouth was slightly parted, the way it always had when she anticipated his kiss, by the way her fabulous green eyes darkened, drawing him in. The signs were subtle, but they were there and he recognized them as clearly as if someone had painted words on a wall.

He chose to dismiss them.

'Stop looking at me like that.' His voice was harsh. Harsher than he'd intended. 'Stop looking as if you want me, when we both know that you'll go after any convenient male body. I happen to prefer my relationships to be exclusive.'

Her beautiful face lost most of its colour. 'How can you say that to me?'

Innocent. Wronged. All those words came to mind as he looked at her and yet he knew none of them applied to her.

There had been nothing innocent about her when he'd caught her naked in their bed with another man.

'Because it's the truth.' Rico gritted his teeth. She managed to make him feel guilty even though he knew that he had nothing to feel guilty about.

Hadn't he caught her red-handed? Filling her days with the pleasures of the flesh when he was working? Spending her evenings in unsavoury nightclubs and taking his young, impressionable sister with her.

'You're looking at me, too. So what does that make you?' Her voice was a choke and he frowned slightly, unsure what to make of her uncharacteristic response. He'd seen the tears in the hospital and had been surprised by how much the sight had bothered him. He knew how tough she was, knew that Stasia wasn't a woman to dissolve into tears.

It must be the awkwardness of their current situation, he decided. Being forced to face him, after the ultimate betrayal. *The tears of a guilty conscience?*

'If I'm looking at you then it's because I can't quite believe I was ever foolish enough to marry you,' he said cruelly, watching her flinch and wondering why it felt so necessary to hurt her when it was supposedly all in the past. When his relationships had gone wrong in the past he'd always been content to walk away. Partings had usually been amicable, invariably smoothed by elaborate gifts on his part, selected to soothe the guilt of not caring enough. But never had he felt this driven, burning need to strike out and inflict pain as he did with Stasia.

'I *hate* you.' She spoke the words on a soft gasp and for a moment he thought he'd misheard and it took him a moment to respond.

'Maybe. But like it or not, you also want me and that's something you're finding it difficult to live with.' He saw her take a step backwards and suddenly he wished she'd worn something, anything, other than his shirt. It was as if she was mocking him. Those glorious legs bared to mid-thigh, the buttons undone to reveal the darkened hollow between her full breasts. She had a body designed to drive a man wild.

And he should know.

She'd driven him out of his mind.

He looked at her expectantly, feeling the charged atmosphere, waiting for her to fight back. Wasn't that what they'd always done? Fought and argued? He was used to women who fawned and agreed with him and Stasia had never done either. She'd challenged him. Had driven him crazy. Had infuriated him as much as she'd excited him.

But tonight it was as if the fight had been sucked out of her.

She stood by his pool, wearing his shirt, looking very young and very lost. 'I didn't come to fight with you.' She raked a hand through her gorgeous, fiery mane in a gesture he knew painfully well. She sounded tired and more uncertain than he could ever remember her sounding before. 'I heard a noise and I wanted to check who it was. And when I saw it was you I wanted to ask you about Chiara. You said you'd be staying at the hospital.' Her voice sounded dull. Strangely devoid of emotion. 'Has there been any change?'

'No change.'

And he realized that since Stasia had appeared on the terrace he hadn't given his sister a thought.

What sort of a man did that make him? he asked himself bitterly.

Disgusted with himself, he turned away from her and strode into the spacious villa, suddenly overwhelmed by the ever-building tension of the past two weeks. He hadn't had a full night's sleep in all that time and his normally sharp brain was definitely seeing the world out of focus.

He sprawled on to the nearest sofa and closed his eyes, feeling less in control than ever in his life before and deciding that it was *not* a feeling he relished.

'Rico—'

He felt the sofa dip next to him, felt the tentative touch of her fingers against the hard muscle of his shoulder.

This was a different Stasia.

A soft, gentle Stasia and this new side of her slid under his skin and increased the torment, like grains of sand in a raw wound.

Her light, subtle perfume teased his senses and he turned to face her, intending to dismiss her concern, to send her back to bed with a few cold words.

But something in her incredible green eyes held him silent.

'This must be terrible for you,' she said quietly, 'and maybe it's time to admit that you have feelings too.

Everyone leans on you. What they forget is that you need someone to lean on, too.'

He wished she'd move her hand from his shoulder. The gentle touch of her fingers seemed to connect to every male part of himself and he suddenly realized just how much he'd missed her touch.

He suppressed a groan and tried to drag his wayward libido back under control. 'I'm just tired. I've been at the hospital for over two weeks—'

'Being strong for everyone. Making decisions for everyone. You need to think about yourself, Rico. About your own needs.'

It was the wrong thing to say. At the moment only one need filled his mind and as he lifted his eyes to hers he remembered just how much this woman knew about his needs.

Mutual desire, dangerous and destructive, flared hot between them and he fought the urge to bury his face in her neck and taste her soft skin. She was all female. All temptation to the male in him, and suddenly he wanted her so badly it was like a fire inside him.

It wasn't clear who made the first move. Wasn't clear when her gentle grip on his arm turned from comfort to something else entirely. Something sexual. Either way, one moment they were apart, locked together in a visual intimacy which stirred all the senses, and the next his mouth was on hers—hot and demanding, taking, stealing, robbing her of breath and protest.

Or maybe there never was a protest. He felt her slender arms wind round his neck, responded to the scrape of her fingernails down his back with a violent shudder. It was primitive and basic, a primal expression of sexual desire that seized them both.

Needing to dominate, he pressed her back on the sofa, staking his claim, satisfying the clawing, greedy beast that had been devouring him since she'd opened the door of her cottage and glared at him with those daredevil don't-mess-with-me green eyes. He forgot the fact that he was torn with worry, that he was mentally and physically exhausted. He forgot everything except the thundering, driving force of his own libido and the fact that he was with the only woman he'd ever wanted to be with.

Without lifting his mouth from hers he swiftly dealt with the buttons of the shirt she was wearing. His shirt. Or was it her shirt now? His usually sharp mind was no longer working properly. Certainly it smelt of her. That subtle, floral, feminine scent that teased his nostrils and other more distant parts of him. That scent that was totally Stasia.

He stroked a possessive hand over the swell of her breasts, her gasp of pleasure sending another thud of answering desire straight to his groin. Then he dragged his mouth away from hers so that he could look, his eyes feasting on the pale softness of her skin that seemed even paler set against the bronze of his own flesh. He'd always been fascinated by the contrast between them. Fragility against strength. English pallor against Mediterranean dark. *Soft woman against hard male.*

Her dusky-pink nipples jutted upwards, tempting, begging, and he bent his dark head and answered her silent plea, sucking her into the moist heat of his mouth, flicking with his tongue until he felt her arch her hips and sink her fingers into his hair. Lost in a sensual feast, he refused to release her and he heard her sob his name and arch again as his tongue flicked with relentless skill and expertise, driving her higher and higher.

And he knew this woman so well.

Knew just how to touch and tempt to send her hurtling towards the edge.

For a moment he was the master, the one in control. And then he felt her fingers on the towel, felt the gentle tug as she unwrapped him, followed by the breath of cool air on his flesh. And he remembered that she knew him too. And she used that knowledge as she covered him with her hand and took the control right back.

Her touch drew a thickened groan from him, an involuntary acknowledgement of what this woman did to him. The way they connected. It would have gone all the way. The way it had from their very first date. Once they started there was no stopping, their mutual passion totally beyond control. But the time wasn't theirs and as usual it was his phone that came between them— that small, seemingly innocent gadget that always seemed to rip holes in their time together.

They froze, locked in intimacies that had come so naturally and which now seemed so shocking and inappropriate.

With a soft curse, Rico sprang to his feet and reached for the towel, securing it quickly before answering the phone with one impatient stab of his finger.

CHAPTER FOUR

'SHE's awake?' Stasia struggled to sit up, her tangled hair forming a curtain over her flushed, mortified face. How could she have done that? Her whole body hummed with sexual frustration and utter humiliation.

She hadn't even meant to follow him into the room, but then she'd seen him slumped on the sofa looking utterly done in and something had ached inside her. And that same something had made her cross the room and offer comfort. But she should have known that it wasn't safe.

One touch.

One touch and she'd lain down for him like the pathetic groupie she was never going to be. Did she have no pride? No will-power? *No sense of self-preservation?* The way to get over Riccardo Crisanti was *not* by allowing him unlimited access to her body.

But being back in the villa, where they'd been so blissfully happy, had made her vulnerable. Weepy. Weak and pathetic. And when she'd seen him, so gloriously naked, a man designed to tempt woman, she'd been unable to maintain the angry front.

'She recovered consciousness five minutes ago.' There was no missing the tension in his voice and she suspected that it wasn't all due to concern for his sister. She wasn't blind. She could see the proud jut of his arousal under the totally insubstantial towel. Knew that he was still throbbing with unfulfilled need.

As she was.

The sexual frustration was so agonizingly acute that she could have screamed with it.

He looked at her, his dark jaw set hard. 'We need to get back to the hospital.' His eyes slid to the swell of her creamy breasts, streaked red from the scrape of his stubble. He turned away as if he couldn't stand the reminder of his own weakness. 'Cover yourself.'

'Damn you, Rico!' Her voice was hoarse as she struggled to do up buttons with shaking fingers. 'I won't let you blame me for this!'

How dared he look at her like that when he'd been every bit as responsible as she for what had flared up between them?

'You came out here dressed only in a shirt.'

'You were naked!'

His gaze was hard. 'Perhaps you think that offering sex makes me more inclined towards forgiveness.'

Offering sex?

'I don't need your forgiveness, Rico—' her voice was hoarse '—but you may well need mine. Get out.'

They glared at each other, neither prepared to take responsibility for the fact that they had a complete inability to be together and not make love. Both refusing to acknowledge the fact that the sexual chemistry between them was such a powerful force that it was outside their control, the pull between them as natural as breathing.

'Willingly.' He stared at her for a moment longer, a tiny pulse beating in his hard jaw, his eyes dangerously dark as he punched a number into his phone and ordered the car to be brought round. 'Get dressed. We're leaving in five minutes.'

And with that he strode out of the room, giving her

a final view of his broad bronzed shoulders and long muscular legs.

For a moment Stasia just sat there staring after him, despising herself for wishing he'd turn round, come back to her and finish what he'd started.

She gave a groan and resisted the temptation to drum her heels into the sofa.

At that particular moment she didn't know who she hated more. Rico, for losing his ice-cool control whenever he came near her or herself, for wanting him every bit as much as he clearly wanted her.

Her only consolation was that Rico hated losing control almost as much as she did. And if she was suffering then there was no doubt that he was suffering too.

And at the moment she really, *truly*, wanted him to suffer. If he felt only one portion of the agony that she was feeling then that would go some way towards satisfying her sense of justice.

She wrapped the shirt around her and padded silently to the sanctuary of her bedroom where she stupidly risked a glance in the mirror. It was a mistake. Her reflection stared back, mocking her. She didn't see the woman she wanted to see. She wanted to see smooth and sleek. She wanted to see calm and control. Instead she saw wild and wanton. Her fiery hair fell around her face in soft tangles, hair that had very evidently been severely disturbed by a rampant male. Her pale, sensitive skin showed all the evidence of his uncompromising sexual demands. Demands that she'd met, bite for bite, lick for lick.

Oh, God.

She covered her swollen lips with shaking fingers.

She should never have come.

She was a strong, independent woman with a mind

of her own and a successful career, but Rico was like a dangerous drug. She couldn't be close to him and not want him and she despised herself for that weakness.

They were as far apart in their attitudes as North was from South but still it seemed she couldn't resist him.

She'd never get over him unless she could put distance between them.

And now that Chiara was awake she was going to do just that.

She was going to make the required visit to the teenager's sickbed, make the right noises and then vanish back to England and find a cottage with such low ceilings that Rico wouldn't be able to gain access without risking extreme physical damage.

As the car sped towards the hospital Rico sat in brooding silence, his mind and body throbbing with an unrelieved sexual tension that did absolutely nothing for his temper.

He couldn't bring himself to look at her.

Couldn't bring himself to focus on the visible signs of his earlier lack of will-power. When he'd dragged her beneath him in a state of sexual desperation, he'd given no thought to the immediate future. To the fact that her delicate skin always displayed the evidence of his attentions for several hours after they'd touched.

The fact that her pale skin was so sensitive had always been a point of fascination for a man whose own skin simply turned a deeper shade of bronze on exposure to the sun. By contrast, the slightest touch of the sun and her skin turned pink and her freckles increased. Worshipping her creamy pallor, he'd made it his mission to protect her, buying her a selection of hats designed to permanently shade her from the powerful Italian sun.

But tonight he'd thought about nothing but his own satisfaction. And now, he reflected grimly, he was about to pay the price for that display of reckless masculine self-indulgence.

In less than ten minutes they'd be meeting his family and he'd be on the receiving end of horrified, questioning glances from his mother.

Questions that he didn't want to answer.

Questions that he *couldn't* answer.

He had absolutely no idea why he behaved with such total lack of control with Stasia. In all other matters he considered himself to be a strictly disciplined man. He'd learned the benefits of self-control at an early age. But with Stasia he reverted to hormone-laden, sex-driven teenager. Unfortunately mind over matter didn't come into it. In his case it was libido over brain.

It was just the stress, he assured himself. A purely physical release from the relentless pressure of the past few days. It didn't mean anything. He was human, after all, and she'd offered comfort.

Was it his fault if the sort of comfort he preferred involved being horizontal?

He stared out of the window and gritted his teeth, aware of her sitting only inches away from him, her bubbling curls pinned in a haphazard style on the back of her head, her curvaceous body once more concealed by the peach linen dress.

But it didn't matter whether she was dressed or naked.

The sexual pull between them was stronger than both of them and the sooner he sent her back to England and delegated communication to his lawyers, the safer for both of them.

He'd give her time to visit his sister, just in case her presence would in any way speed Chiara's recovery, and then he'd have her taken straight to his plane.

And he'd make sure that the engines were already running.

The whole family was standing by Chiara's bedside and Stasia felt her heart plummet. After her steamy, heated encounter with Rico she felt more vulnerable than ever and was well aware that, despite her best efforts with make-up, she was displaying signs of his attentions for all who looked.

She wanted to sink through the floor with humiliation.

Even more so when she met Rico's mother's shocked gaze.

'So—you have come back.' His mother's voice was stiff and her eyes scanned Stasia's heightened colour, rested on her bruised mouth and then shifted to her son with a look of undisguised horror and disbelief.

Eternally indifferent to the opinion of others, Rico met his mother's reproachful gaze with admirable cool and took Stasia's hand, openly defying anyone to challenge him. Then he stepped towards the bed, leaving no one in any doubt about who was in charge.

Pathetically grateful to him for his gesture of protection, even though she knew that it meant nothing, Stasia held his hand as though it were a lifeline.

His mother stepped back respectfully but the glance she gave Stasia was so pained that the younger woman felt a lump building in her throat. What had she ever done to deserve that look? Nothing. Except marry a billionaire. Apparently that had been enough to earn her the label of 'gold-digger.'

'Chiara—' Rico's voice was roughened with concern as he bent to kiss his sister.

Her eyes fluttered open and for a moment she stared at her brother blankly. Then a smile touched her mouth.

'Rico.' Her voice was little more than a whisper but the entire family released a collective sigh of relief. Rico's mother stepped forward and embraced her daughter, and Chiara's grandmother sank into a chair by the bed and took her hand, tears pouring down her wrinkled cheeks.

'She's come back to us—'

Which sounded like Stasia's cue to leave.

Without even realizing that she was doing so, she freed her hand from Rico's and backed towards the door.

She wasn't needed here. She wasn't part of their family and never had been. Chiara had regained consciousness. It was time to go home.

But Chiara was saying something else, her voice so hushed that Rico had to bend his dark head closer in order to hear her.

He straightened and his gaze arrowed in on Stasia who by now was by the door, preparing to leave. 'Wait.' His voice was roughened by emotion. 'She's wondering where you are. She wants to speak to you.'

Stasia froze. For a moment she thought she must have misheard him. Why on earth would Chiara want to speak to her now that she had fully regained consciousness? Uttering her name in a semi-comatose state was one thing but this was something quite different.

Aware that the whole family was looking at her,

Stasia swallowed and released her hold on the door handle.

After all, what could Chiara say that she hadn't already said? What could she do to hurt her that she hadn't already done?

Feeling the increased beat of her heart, she walked towards the bed, every step a supreme effort of will.

Rico stood to one side as she approached and she stared down at Chiara, noticing that the bruise on her forehead seemed even more livid.

'Hello, Chiara.' Her voice was little more than a croak. 'I'm so glad you're awake. We've all been worried.'

'Stasia.' Chiara gave a soft smile and her eyes drifted shut. 'Beautiful Stasia. When I'm better, can we go shopping? You always look so fabulous. I want you to teach me how to dress like you.'

There was a shocked, disbelieving silence from all those gathered around the bed.

Stasia stood rigid, unsure how to respond. She and Rico had lived apart for the whole of the past year. Why would Chiara say a thing like that, unless she was trying to drive the knife in the moment she regained consciousness? She searched Chiara's face, looking for signs of the mockery she knew so well, the defiance and sarcasm that had been so much a part of the girl when she'd known her, but they were missing.

Chiara's eyes opened and she glanced around her, trying to interpret the silence. She looked wary. Puzzled. As if she sensed that something was wrong.

'What's the matter? Wh—what have I said?'

'Nothing, *mia piccola*,' Rico was quick to reassure her, his hand covering hers. 'How are you feeling?'

Chiara winced slightly. 'I have a headache. And I don't understand why you're all here. What happened?'

'I told you about the accident.' Rico's dark brows locked in a frown. 'You don't remember the accident?'

Chiara thought for a moment and then shook her head slightly. 'Nothing. I just remember that you're on your honeymoon.' She gave her brother a wobbly smile. 'And you were really mad at me for turning up unannounced and disturbing your romantic twosome. Are you still mad at me or am I forgiven?'

Rico looked as though he'd been turned to stone, his powerful body motionless. Standing close to him, Stasia felt his tension and heard his mother's murmur of concern from the other side of the bed. She did a swift mental calculation and worked out that the incident that Chiara was referring to had occurred almost a year and a half ago. At the beginning of their honeymoon.

Before they'd had time to recognize their insurmountable differences.

So what did that mean? Was Chiara playing yet more games?

Chiara's smile faltered and she glanced between them, sensing something in the atmosphere. 'Rico? Are you still angry with me?'

'No, *piccola*, I'm not angry.' Rico's eyes flickered over his sister's face, as if searching for clues. 'But is that the last thing you remember? Arriving when Stasia and I were on our honeymoon?'

Chiara nodded. 'Why?'

Rico smiled. 'No reason.' His deep voice was strong and reassuring and betrayed none of the worry that he was clearly feeling. 'I need to talk to the doctors again. Try and rest. Don't worry about anything.'

The doctors gathered round the bed at Rico's bidding

and the family retreated to the relatives' room for yet another tense wait.

They didn't wait long. Within minutes Rico was called back to the bedside and he returned to the waiting room moments later, looking more stressed than Stasia could ever remember seeing him before.

'The doctors say that she has amnesia. Memory loss.' His eyes slid to his mother as he spoke, checking her reaction to the news. 'Apparently it's common. She can remember nothing since that day when she turned up at the villa when Stasia and I—' he broke off and then continued with what appeared to be considerable effort '—Stasia and I were on our honeymoon.'

Stasia felt her colour rise as everyone turned to look at her.

She remembered that day so well.

They'd been on the beach, swimming and making love endlessly. When they'd finally dragged themselves back to the villa, still locked in each other's arms, Chiara had been in the pool.

Rico had been furious with his sister and Stasia had gently intervened, although she too had been disappointed to find that suddenly they had company.

In the end Rico had heeded Stasia's pleas and allowed Chiara to stay for the weekend and had then dispatched her back to school with a severe lecture about concentrating on her studies.

Stasia let out a breath, realizing that if this was the last thing that Chiara could remember then she was missing a substantial chunk of her life.

Shocked by the news of this new complication, his mother sank into the nearest chair, a look of horror on her face. 'Is it permanent?'

Rico gave a shrug that made him seem more Sicilian

than ever. 'They cannot say. There's every probability that her memory will return but no one knows when. In the immediate term the priority is her physical recovery. They are extremely pleased with her progress. All being well she should be able to come home to us in a few days, which is nothing short of a miracle.'

His mother smiled with relief, her hands clasped in her lap. 'You will take her to your villa?'

Rico gave a nod. 'She needs peace and a restful atmosphere. The villa is the obvious place. I'll make arrangements to work from Sicily for the time being so that I can keep an eye on her.'

'I will come and stay also and take care of her,' his mother said immediately but Rico shook his head.

'There's no need. She needs to be kept as quiet as possible. It would be far better if you stayed in your home and visited from time to time.'

His mother gave a reluctant nod. 'If you think it's best.'

As usual she deferred to Rico, as did the entire family.

When Stasia had first met them their total dependence on him for every decision had astonished her and then later it had driven her crazy. Weren't any of the women in his family capable of thinking and acting for themselves, without his permission?

Stasia glanced at her watch and realized that it would be dawn soon. 'Well, it's clear that I'm no longer needed,' she said quietly, her eyes sliding to Rico, trying to subdue the desire to throw herself at him. *Trying not to think that this was probably the last time she'd ever see him.* From now on it would be back to the lawyers.

The reality of that fact left her feeling profoundly depressed.

'I'm afraid it isn't that simple.' Rico's expression was grim, as if he were dealing with an issue that he found distinctly unpalatable. 'Unfortunately, Chiara's memory is locked at that point eighteen months ago when we were on our honeymoon. She thinks we're happily married.'

Stasia took a long, slow breath. That fact hadn't escaped her. 'Then, I suppose, at some point you'll just have to tell her that we've been living apart for the past year.' But not the reason why. Only she and Chiara knew the truth and Chiara no longer had a memory. 'You'll have to tell her the truth.'

What choice did they have? At some point Chiara would presumably seek an explanation as to why they were no longer living together.

'In this case the truth is not an option.' The words were dragged out of him and he looked like a man who was well and truly stuck between a rock and a hard place. 'The doctors are insistent that she should have no shocks. That everything around her should be as calm as possible. She shouldn't be subjected to any stress.'

So what exactly was he suggesting?

Stasia gave a short laugh that held not a trace of humour. 'And we both know that Chiara was hardly devastated by the failure of our marriage, Rico. Let's not play games here. She was delighted when our relationship failed. Being reminded of the truth is hardly going to send her into a decline.'

Rico's mother made a sound of protest but neither Stasia or Rico spared her a glance.

It was as if they were the only two people in the

room, their eyes locked together as the conflict built between them.

'Unfortunately for us, Chiara is living at a different point of our relationship,' Rico growled, everything about his body language suggesting that he was finding this whole situation as difficult as she was. 'And we are *not* going over old ground again now. *Dio*, do you think we don't have enough stress at the moment without dredging up bad feeling from the past?'

Her heart started to beat more rapidly. 'So what are you suggesting?' Fuelled by nerves that she didn't understand, Stasia couldn't keep the sarcasm out of her tone. 'You want to play happy families? You want to put that wedding ring back on my finger?'

There was a long pulsing silence and then Rico released a long breath. 'If that's what it takes, then yes.'

CHAPTER FIVE

STASIA stared at him in shocked silence. That was the one response that she had *not* expected. Finally she found her voice. 'You *can't* be serious.'

'*Dio*, would I joke about such a thing? My lawyers have virtually completed the paperwork necessary for the divorce. Do you think I want to prolong it?'

If he'd intended to hurt her then he succeeded admirably.

Even his mother looked slightly startled by his lack of tact.

To give him his due, Rico swore softly and ran a hand over the back of his neck, fighting for control. 'That was uncalled for and I apologize,' he muttered and Stasia tossed her head back, her hair gleaming like a beacon under the bright hospital lights.

'For what, Rico? Being yourself?' She would have died rather than let him see the effect he had on her still. Died rather than let him see that he had the ability to wound her deeply. 'But I think your reaction more than proves that your suggestion is utterly ridiculous. You can put the ring back on my finger but we'll never act like two people who love each other. It's a totally ridiculous proposition.'

With a grim expression on his handsome face, Rico turned his gaze on his family. 'Chiara would like some company.'

He didn't order them to leave but his meaning was

perfectly clear. He wanted to talk to Stasia without an audience.

They left like lambs, no one daring to question him. They never questioned him.

Stasia watched them leave in incredulous disbelief and then turned to him, eyes blazing. 'Do you know your problem?'

'No—' Rico caught her gaze with burning black eyes every bit as mocking as her own '—but I feel sure that you're about to tell me.'

She ignored the warning in his silky tone. Ignored the signs that indicated the slow build of his temper. 'No one has ever said "no" to you. You stride through life, always the one in control, always the one making decisions, crashing through obstacles like a bull. Well, I've got news for you—' she drew several short breaths, trying to get air into her starving lungs '—I am *not* one of your pathetic groupies who hang around with their tongues hanging out, just waiting to be given a morsel of attention from your illustrious self. I'm not one of those irritating, perfectly groomed women who say "yes" to you all the time.'

He stepped towards her so quickly that she didn't see it coming. 'We both know that I can make you say "yes" any time I please, *cara mia*.'

'Don't call me that.'

Conscious of his superior height and every inch of his throbbing masculinity, her heart pounded and she took a step backwards, then wished she hadn't when she caught the sardonic lift of his black brows.

'Afraid of me, Stasia?' He stepped closer, the movement deliberate and designed to provoke. 'Or are you moving away because you don't trust yourself to resist me?'

He was just *so* arrogant. So maddeningly sure of himself.

'I'm not afraid—I just don't approve of men who use their size to intimidate women. It's a low trick.'

He threw back his head and laughed in genuine amusement, a rich, dark sound that coiled around her insides and cranked the tension even higher. 'You expect me to believe that I intimidate you? You, with your sharp tongue and those flashing eyes that dare me all the time? Tell me one thing that you're afraid of. Just one thing!'

Stasia swallowed. *Her own feelings.*

She was afraid of her own feelings for him. They were totally at odds with the person she was. Or the person she believed herself to be. She wasn't a clingy person. She despised clingy people. Unfortunately, since meeting Rico, she'd made the painful discovery that there were parts of her that she'd never known existed. *Sensual depths that he'd plundered like a master.* And with him she wanted to cling. Cling and never let go.

'This is getting us nowhere.' She licked dry lips and then regretted the gesture instantly as his gaze dropped to her mouth and his eyes gleamed gold. That look was as familiar to her as the insidious melting sensation in the pit of her stomach that followed. She rejected the feeling instantly. 'But it has proved that we can't remain in the same room and not want to kill each other. Unless Chiara has lost her intuition as well as her memory then there is no way we'll convince her that our relationship is genuine. I'll say goodbye to her and then I'm leaving.'

'You're not going anywhere,' he said silkily, 'and if

you're worried that we can't convince Chiara that we're in love, then let me help you out on that one.'

She should have seen it coming. Should have sensed his intention before he acted. But her brain was foggy and thinking suddenly seemed impossibly hard work. Even more so when his hand snaked round her waist and his mouth came down on hers with the assurance of a man totally confident in his own sexuality and her response to him.

As kisses went it was as skilled as it was brief. He controlled and led, coaxing her lips apart with a teasing flick of his tongue, delving inside in a lazy exploration that promised so much more than it delivered. And, just as he'd intended, he set her on fire.

He drove her higher, to the point where she forgot everything. She forgot where they were. Forgot that they were standing in an impersonal waiting room illuminated by harsh lighting with his sister seriously ill nearby. Forgot their differences, the fact that they seemed to have absolutely no common ground except between the sheets.

All she was aware of was *him*. The scrape of masculine stubble against her sensitive skin, the suggestive lick of his tongue and the bold thrust of his manhood pressed against the burning heat of her pelvis. Sexual tension throbbed and vibrated through her whole body and her arms crept around his neck, drawing him closer still.

And then he ended it.

With humiliating ease, he lifted his head and stepped back, his eyes cold and totally lacking in emotion. 'I think that's enough to prove that we can be fairly convincing when the time comes.'

She swayed dizzily, just *hating* him for being so controlled when she felt so completely out of control.

His dark eyes registered her dazed expression with something approaching insolence. 'You like to think you don't need me, Stasia, but we both know that you'll lie down for me whenever I like, so it's useless pretending otherwise.'

The sharp sound of her hand connecting with his cheek echoed round the small room.

'You are a smug, conceited bastard, Rico,' she said shakily, hugging her stinging hand to her chest, shocked by the unaccustomed violence which had erupted inside her at his callous taunt. Up until this moment she'd never struck another human being in her life but Rico was hurting her all over again. 'And I'm not staying here a moment longer. Please instruct your pilot to make whatever preparations he needs to make to fly me home.'

'You're not going home.' His lean cheek displayed the livid mark made by her hand and his black eyes glittered dangerously.

'You asked me to come when Chiara was in a coma. Well, now she's awake so you don't need me any more.'

His jaw tightened. 'I've already explained why I need you.'

'To be your convenient slut?' Her eyes blazed into his. 'I don't think so, Rico. There are millions of women out there just gagging to fill that role. Go and grab one of them instead.'

'I want you to be my wife for however long it takes for Chiara to regain her memory,' he growled, digging his hands in his pockets, as if he were afraid of what he might do with them if they were allowed continued freedom. 'But being my wife is not something you ever excelled at, was it, Stasia? I gave you everything. You had a lifestyle beyond your wildest dreams, but when I returned home from a long working day, expecting to find my wife waiting for me, I found her gone!'

'Twice! Twice I was away. I had a business to run too!'

'For what purpose?' His careless shrug betrayed his complete lack of insight into her character. 'You didn't need the money. You had access to unlimited funds. You had everything a woman could possibly need.'

Except love.

She spread her hands in a gesture of exasperation. 'Money, money, money! Life isn't always about money, Rico. There are other things that matter, like independence and self-belief. I like my work. I need to know that I'm good at something. Making a contribution that matters.'

'You were good in my bed,' he said softly, his eyes fixed on hers, 'and that was what mattered to me.'

Her cheeks flamed and she dragged her eyes away from his with an exclamation of disgust. 'You are totally primitive, Rico! You didn't want a wife. You wanted a mistress.'

'I already had two mistresses before I married you,' he said icily, his tone bored and his dark eyes never shifting from hers. 'Why would I have wanted a third?'

Her face lost the rest of its colour at that stark reminder of the man she'd taken on. Had lost her heart to. She'd been crazy to think that what she felt for him would ever be returned. Rico didn't know what love was. He wasn't capable of connecting with a woman emotionally. Only physically. He had an almost insatiable sex drive. She'd heard rumours that he had a mistress both in Rome and in Paris but at the time she'd chosen to ignore those rumours. Rico was a drop-dead sexy guy and she didn't for one minute expect him to have lived like a monk.

'As usual, our conversations lead us nowhere,' she said flatly, picking her bag up from the chair and slinging it over her shoulder. 'I'm leaving, Rico, and there's nothing you can do to stop me. If you won't let me use your plane then I'll just get a commercial flight.'

Anything to get away from him.

At this point she was so desperate that she would have chartered her own plane if that were the only option remaining to guarantee her escape.

'The only place you're going is back to the villa to play happy families.'

'I'm not a member of your staff, nor am I any longer a member of your family,' she said tartly, 'so I don't follow orders.'

'You never did,' he said coldly, 'but you're still going to do as I say.'

'And by what means do you intend to coerce me?' She tilted her head to one side, her expression blatantly challenging. 'Thumb screws? The rack?'

'I don't have to resort to anything so crude,' he replied evenly. 'I merely have to instruct the bank to foreclose on the loan for your mother's antique shop. One phone call, Stasia. That's all it would take.'

There was a long silence, broken only by the sound of Stasia's rapid breathing. When she finally spoke her voice was far from steady. 'You can't do that. You shouldn't even know about that.' She shook her head slightly, denying the possibility that he was telling the truth. 'That loan is nothing to do with you.'

He looked bored. 'Now who is being naïve, Stasia?

Why do you think the bank agreed to the loan so easily?'

She stared at him. 'It *wasn't* easy. We presented sound business plans—'

'Which were ambitious,' Rico said smoothly, 'and the loan was granted because I agreed to act as guarantor.'

'That isn't true.' *Dear God, don't let it be true.* 'You're lying.'

His gaze didn't waver. 'Phone the bank.'

Her mind was racing through all the possibilities, examining the facts. 'But I applied for the loan in my mother's name. I didn't mention you.'

'You were my wife and I have a great deal of trouble remaining anonymous, as you should know by now,' he said dryly. 'Some hotshot at the bank recognized you from the papers. After that they were only too pleased to help you in any way they could.'

With dawning horror, Stasia remembered how the staff at the bank had gone from being condescending and downright obstructive to obsequious. At the time she'd confidently assumed it was because they'd given her business plan proper consideration. Now she cringed at her naïvety.

How could she have been so stupid? How could she not have suspected that her relationship with Rico was behind the sudden change in attitude? Hadn't she seen it before a million times? The way people fawned over Rico, doing anything to win his approval.

'No.' She closed her eyes, wanting it not to be true, but knowing that it was. Suddenly her legs felt ridiculously shaky and she felt physically sick. 'I never wanted that. I never wanted to take anything from you.'

Or she would have become exactly what his family had thought she was. *A gold-digger.*

The thought appalled her. She wanted to achieve things on her own merits. And she'd never been interested in Rico's money. Just in him. *The man himself.*

She stared at him, uncomprehending. 'Why?' Her voice cracked slightly. 'Why did you do that? We weren't even together—'

His handsome face was blank of expression. 'Call it compensation,' he drawled, 'payment for services rendered.'

She turned away so that he couldn't see the pain on her face. Payment. He saw everything in terms of money, including their relationship. And that attitude explained why, for the entire duration of their marriage, she'd felt like his mistress. Never his wife. He'd showered her with gifts and extravagant jewellery, as if money could compensate for the deficiencies in their relationship. It was the only form of currency that he understood.

'I mean it, Stasia,' he drawled with deadly emphasis. 'Either you stay and play the part of the loving wife until such time as I decide that Chiara is well enough or I close down your business. I can and will do it.'

She looked at him with loathing. 'I can't believe that even you could stoop so low.'

'Your opinion on the matter is totally irrelevant.' He was totally unmoved by her passionate declaration and she curled her fists into her palms to stop herself striking him again.

'If you do *anything* to hurt my mother—'

'The decision whether or not to hurt your mother lies in *your* hands,' he pointed out, his tone silky smooth. 'Agree to stay as my wife for as long as it takes Chiara to regain her memory and the loan is secure. When we finally divorce I shall make sure the business is yours.'

She swallowed hard, her gaze filled with contempt as she considered the position he was putting her in. He was leaving her with absolutely no choice and he knew it. 'You are utterly ruthless—'

'When I want something, then I go after it until I get it. If that's ruthless then yes, I'm ruthless.' He gave a dismissive shrug that showed how little the accusation troubled him and she turned away in disgust, knowing that he'd applied exactly that philosophy in his pursuit of her.

He'd wanted her and he'd been prepared to go to any lengths in order to have her.

'Why are you doing this?' Her voice was little more than a whisper. 'Our marriage was a disaster. We both know that. Why would you want me back?'

They'd had no contact for over a year.

Surely he couldn't be asking this of her.

His brief glance revealed the depth of his contempt for her. 'I don't want you back. But Chiara needs a stable environment. Until her memory recovers, she needs to be protected from shocks. And our marriage was *not* a disaster.' His eyes glittered dangerously in his handsome face. 'But you were too stubborn to allow it to work, too fiercely independent to accept that marriage is a partnership. And I won't have Chiara punished for your failings in that direction. I don't want her to know that our relationship is over.'

For a moment Stasia just stared at him blankly, astonished by his accusation. *He* was telling *her* that marriage was a partnership? That *she* was stubborn? When all the compromises had been hers—

She shook her head, uncomprehending. 'I can't believe you'd do this to me. To yourself.'

Because this had to be hurting him too.

She could read his distaste for the task in every angle of his sharp, masculine features, in the way he kept his powerful body at a safe distance from hers. As if to come too close might contaminate him.

Stasia gazed at him helplessly. No wonder he was such a successful businessman. Like the most dangerous predator, he looked for the weakness in his prey and then used that weakness to achieve his own ends. How could she have fallen in love with a man like him? How could she have been so blinded to the person he was? How could she have ever thought that this man might be capable of so gentle an emotion as love? 'It isn't a practical solution, Rico. I need to work—I have commissions—'

'You can work from the villa.' His black eyes slammed into hers. 'But no travelling. Anything that would take you out of Sicily will have to wait until Chiara's condition allows us to finally reveal the truth.'

She wanted to argue, but how could she when her mother's happiness depended on her compliance? He was leaving her absolutely no choice and he knew it. This wasn't about their relationship, it was about his need to control.

'All right.' She could barely frame the words. 'I'll do it. But don't expect me to like you for this.'

'How times change.' His gaze didn't shift from hers and the sarcasm in his hard tone bit into her flesh. 'I can remember a time when you used to call me on my mobile every hour to beg me to come home and make love to you.'

It was a cruel reminder of just how open she'd been

with him. How honest. She'd never been afraid to tell him how she felt, even though he'd never revealed anything of his own feelings in return.

With the benefit of hindsight she realized that it was because he hadn't shared her feelings. How could he express what he didn't feel?

She lifted her chin, trying to hang on to the last of her pride. 'I never begged.'

'Oh, you begged, Stasia, in that sexy, husky voice of yours—' his own voice was soft and tormenting '—and when I arrived you'd be naked in the bed. Waiting. Waiting for me. *Wanting me.*'

Stasia closed her eyes, just hating the picture he was painting. A picture of a clingy, dependent woman, something she'd always promised herself she'd never become. And that was part of the reason their marriage had failed, of course. She'd never been comfortable with the woman she became when she was with this man.

'I certainly remember the waiting,' she said coldly, making a supreme effort to hold herself together. 'I remember endless days and weeks spent waiting for you to come home from yet another business trip. Sitting there, bored and alone.'

'So boring that you took a lover?'

'That is *not* what happened.'

'Then how else do you explain a naked man in our bedroom? *Our bedroom*?'

A tense silence followed his outburst of raw emotion and her heart almost stopped.

They'd never even talked about what had happened. Incensed by the accusation in his eyes and frantic at the steady destruction of their relationship, she'd walked out, expecting him to follow and demand an explanation. He hadn't.

She lifted an eyebrow. 'You finally want to talk about this? A year after the event? Don't you think it's a bit late?'

He chose to ignore her sarcasm, but streaks of colour highlighted his incredible bone structure, always a warning of impending trouble. 'Did he know how wild you were in bed? How totally insatiable? There's no way a pathetic little guy like that ever would have been able to satisfy your appetite for sex.'

Stasia paled. *Only with him.* He was the only man who'd ever done that to her. The only man she'd ever been to bed with. But then he'd always credited her with more experience than she had. The night he'd discovered that she was a virgin he'd been so shocked that he'd almost been driven to apologize, which would have been a first for Rico Crisanti, a man not given to apologizing for anything.

'*Madre de Dio*, why are we even talking about this?' He raked a hand through his dark hair and snatched a jagged breath. 'I need to get some air or I will do something I regret.'

With a final dangerous glance in her direction that left her in no doubt as to the volatile state of his temper, he strode out of the room, slamming the door behind him.

CHAPTER SIX

CHIARA was allowed home a few days later on the understanding that she rested and was supervised.

Stasia knew that she should feel pleased that the teenager had recovered sufficiently to be discharged from the hospital, but instead her anxiety levels grew.

She and Chiara had spent a fair degree of time together when she had lived in Rome as Rico's wife and it had been a thoroughly stressful experience. She knew that Chiara hated Rico's villa in Sicily, finding it isolated and boring in the extreme. How would they get on, forced to endure what might be weeks in each other's company?

But Chiara, it seemed, was a changed person.

From the moment she arrived at the villa she was pathetically eager to please, determined not to be a nuisance and outwardly charmed by the view from the terrace.

'Do you think I might be able to swim in the sea,' she asked, staring longingly across the private beach to where the ocean sparkled in the summer sunshine.

'Try the pool first,' Rico advised, handing her a hat and gesturing to a sun lounger. 'Sit down and Maria will bring you a drink. And you should probably try and sleep. I need to make a few calls. If you need anything, ask Stasia. I'll see you at dinner.' He brushed his sister's head in an affectionate gesture and then strode off, leaving her staring after him.

'He's always been more of a father to me than a brother,' she murmured and Stasia looked at her warily,

100

unsure how to respond. She knew that, in the past at least, Chiara had hated that fact. Had hated the fact that Rico was so strict with her.

Stasia kept her response neutral. 'He loves you very much.'

Fortunately Chiara fell asleep and the afternoon passed quickly. Stasia went for a wander through the fruit orchards that surrounded the villa, struggling with memories of the first time Rico had brought her here. She'd fallen in love with the island, with the blend of history and culture and the sheer beauty of the scenery. As excited as any tourist, she'd made Rico take her to all the most famous sights and together they'd visited magnificent Greek temples, Norman cathedrals and Baroque palaces until the heat and the sheer volume of people had driven them back to the cool privacy of his villa and more intimate pleasures. But those heady, happy days had given her some insight into what it meant to be Sicilian. And she knew that for Rico it was everything.

Deep in thought, Stasia walked under the trees, picked herself an orange and then returned to the cool, vine-covered terrace. Chiara still slept and Stasia curled up on a sun lounger and lost herself in her sketchbook, enjoying the faint breeze from the sea.

By the time Chiara woke it was time to dress for dinner.

Retiring to the sanctuary of the bedroom she'd been using while Chiara had been in the hospital, Stasia found it stripped bare of her belongings.

Immediately she went and found Rico's housekeeper.

'Your things have been moved to the master suite, *signora*,' the woman told her gravely and Stasia frowned.

Why would Rico have done that?

Feeling decidedly uneasy, Stasia marched to the master bedroom and walked in without bothering to knock just as Rico strolled out of the shower, his glorious bronzed body touched by specks of water, a small towel in his hand as he dried his sleek, dark hair.

Stasia stopped dead and ceased to breathe.

Her eyes feasted on him, taking in his broad shoulders and the powerful swell of his biceps. She bit back a whimper of need as her eyes drifted to his powerful chest. The shadow of dark body hair seemed to intensify his masculinity and guided the greedy female eye down over his board-flat stomach and lower still to his awesome manhood.

Suddenly feeling dizzy, she finally remembered to suck breath into her starving lungs, but she couldn't shift her eyes.

His response to her gaze was instantaneous and shockingly basic but he showed absolutely no embarrassment by his body's blatant arousal. Instead of using the hand towel to preserve his modesty, he threw it carelessly to one side, his eyes fixed on Stasia's face.

'Well, I think if my little sister could see us now, we wouldn't have any trouble convincing her that we're very much together,' he said with a sardonic lift of his black brows.

Stasia jerked as if he'd slapped her, appalled by her own response to him.

She'd stared. Oh, dear God, she'd stared and stared.

She turned away, totally flustered, but he gave a laugh that contained not the slightest trace of humour.

'I think it's a bit late for either of us to pretend indifference,' he drawled, strolling towards her, still gloriously naked. 'The fact that you still do this for me, even knowing what I know about you, says quite a lot about your appeal, *cara mia*.' There was an edge to his voice that suggested that he was far from pleased to discover that she still affected him.

She kept her eyes averted and clasped her hands behind her back so that he wouldn't see that they were shaking. 'Maria said that my things had been moved.' Her voice was husky and suddenly the room seemed airless. 'I wondered why.'

'Why do you think?' He strolled into his dressing room and reached for a T-shirt, pulling it over his head.

Stasia closed her eyes briefly, wishing desperately that he'd started by dressing his lower half.

But what difference did clothes make, anyway? she reasoned helplessly. Whoever said that 'clothes maketh the man' had never met Rico. In his case it was more a case of 'man maketh the clothes.' He turned the softest, most casual T-shirt into a fashion must-have but Stasia knew that he spent virtually no time considering his appearance. He bought the best and then he forgot about clothes. His sophisticated style was more a result of accident and physical perfection than design.

Mockery in his night-dark eyes, he reached for a pair of silk underpants and drew them on, his gaze holding hers, challenging her. 'I would have thought the reason is obvious.' Trousers came next and finally he was fully clothed. Stasia waited for the high frequency buzz of sexual excitement to die down but there seemed to be no relief. Her entire body was on fire for the man.

It was just because she hadn't had sex for a year, she told herself hastily, backing towards the door, trying to ignore the spread of heat low in her pelvis. 'I'll come back later.'

'Of course you will.' His voice was smooth. 'From now on you'll be sleeping in here. Sleeping, dressing— all the things that a normal married couple do in their bedroom.'

She froze. 'You're expecting me to share a room with you?'

'Absolutely.'

'Then you're delusional.' Her heart started to thud. 'There's no way I'm sleeping in here with you.'

He couldn't be serious.

He couldn't—

He walked across the room with a cool sense of purpose. 'Then I call the bank.' He lifted the receiver and she stopped dead.

'No!' Her tone was sharp and she lifted a hand to her forehead as she tried to think clearly. 'Don't do that. Put it down.'

Her heart slumped in her chest as she considered her options. Again he was leaving her no choice. But how was she supposed to share a room with him?

It was the very worst kind of torture.

He replaced the receiver, his eyes fixed on her face. 'From now on, this is your room. Chiara's room is just two doors away. If you don't sleep here, then she'll know.'

She forced herself to breathe. 'I'm *not* sleeping in the bed with you!'

He glanced at his watch, ignoring her passionate statement. 'Dinner is in ten minutes. Don't you need to change?'

She glared at him for a moment and then walked into the dressing room and slammed the door.

Stasia lingered over dinner, prolonging the moment when she would have to return to the bedroom.

Rico's bedroom.

'It will be so great to be at home with you both,' Chiara said happily, helping herself to more olives. 'But I do feel guilty, making you stay here. I know you must be itching to get back to Rome, Rico.'

Stasia jumped as Rico's hand covered hers. 'As it happens this is a perfect time for me to spend some time with Stasia.' Dark velvety eyes caressed hers. 'I have neglected her in the past while I've been working and I intend to rectify that.' He lifted her hand to his lips, his gaze loaded with sensual promise.

To her utter horror, Stasia felt a lump building in her throat. Those were the words he should have spoken when they were married and still together. Not now, when it was too late and just for the benefit of his sister.

Chiara just smiled, ignorant of the undercurrents in the room. 'Well, I promise that I won't get in the way this time. You can be as romantic as you like. You won't even know I'm here.'

Romantic?

Swamped by an excess of emotion, Stasia snatched her hand away from Rico's and dropped her fork. 'I'm sorry—I'm feeling a little tired. I think I'll have an early night.' She ignored Rico's warning glance and rose to her feet. 'I hope you have a good night. I'll see you at breakfast.'

With that she left the room and sought refuge in the bedroom. If there'd been a key she would have locked the door but there wasn't and she knew that it was only a matter of time before Rico joined her.

He strode into the room minutes later, a grim expression on his handsome face as his dark eyes swept over her pale cheeks. 'You'd better work harder on your performance or I'll be making that phone call.'

She sat on the edge of the bed, feeling slightly sick 'Unlike you, I find it hard to live a lie. It's something I need to learn.'

'Then learn quickly,' he advised silkily, 'or the deal is off.'

'I'm trying.'

'You call sitting in silence throughout dinner trying?' Dark brows rose in question. 'You stared at your plate. What happened to the loving looks?'

'I'm working on them.'

'Then work harder and faster. And from now on I want you to talk as you normally do. Silence is *not* your trademark, as we both well know. And I want you to smile. And I want you to act as though you can't keep your hands off me, *cara mia*.'

'Does it count if I strangle you?' Her eyes flashed with some of her old fire and his eyes gleamed in appreciative response.

'Save that for the bedroom,' he suggested with a predatory smile that made him seem more dangerous than ever. 'In public I want you to touch me like a lover.'

She looked at him sickly. 'But I don't want to touch you like a lover.'

'That's a lie, and we both know it,' he said softly, reaching for the hem of his T-shirt in a slow, deliberate gesture designed to torment. He pulled the garment over his head to reveal a bronzed torso that would have made a Greek god groan in envy. 'We may both hate the fact, but the truth is that you and I have never been able to keep our hands off each other. Perhaps you need reminding of that fact.'

She tried to scoot off the bed but he moved with lightning speed, sliding an arm around her waist and preventing her escape.

'Let me go. This wasn't part of our agreement.' Her heart was thudding so hard she thought it would burst and she lifted both hands to his chest, intending to push him away. It was a mistake. The minute the sensitive tips of her fingers made contact with the hair on his chest and the sleek, bronzed skin beneath, she wanted to cling. Desperately she tried to summon up the will-power to free herself from his hold but he was too close. Too tempting. Suddenly she felt dizzy and light-headed.

It had been so long. So long since he'd held her. So long since she'd breathed in that male smell that she found so seductive.

They stayed like that for a moment, poised on the edge of sexual insanity. And then his mouth came down on hers.

It was pure possession. A statement of intent, his tongue immediately demanding access, probing the depths of her mouth with a skill and precision that left her shaking just as he'd known it would. He'd always known exactly how to drive the maximum response from her.

His hands slipped from her waist to her buttocks and he jerked her against him in a primitive male gesture, bringing her burning pelvis into contact with the hard ridge of his arousal. And he held her there. Male against female. Hard against soft. The muscles of his shoulders bunched under her fingers, his mouth plundered and stole and still he held her. Making her aware of what she did to him.

And finally she couldn't stand it any longer. The fire was so intense that she needed relief and he was the only one who could give it. Nothing else mattered.

She groaned into his mouth and he tipped her backwards on to the bed and came down on top of her, removing the rest of his clothes so swiftly that she wasn't even aware that he'd undressed until she felt the shockingly delicious feel of his naked body against hers.

His eyes fixed on hers, his expression one of grim purpose, he stripped her quickly and then spread her legs for his heated gaze.

She made an embarrassed protest but he ignored her,

sliding a warm, leisurely hand from the soft swell of her breast down to the cluster of bright curls that should have hidden her femininity. But he wasn't allowing her to hide. His eyes held hers, increasing the intimacy as his fingers explored her most sensitive flesh with erotic precision.

And it felt wickedly good.

So good that when he gave a low laugh of masculine triumph she didn't even hear him. And if she had heard she wouldn't have cared. She was totally focused on the moment and what he was doing to her body.

She closed her eyes and moved against his hand, past hearing, past reacting to anything except the sensations that he was creating throughout her totally responsive body.

And when she opened her eyes again he was looking at her, thick dark lashes shielding his expression as he witnessed her total unrestrained surrender to his masterly touch.

When it came, her climax was so intense that she dug her nails into his shoulders and cried out his name so sharply that he lowered his head and kissed her deeply, taking the sobs and gasps into his mouth, smothering the sound. It went on and on and his fingers stayed deep inside her, drawing every last ounce of response from her quivering body.

When the last pulses of her sexual peak died away he lifted his head, but still didn't move his hand, his eyes slightly mocking as he surveyed her hectically flushed cheeks and her parted lips.

'You always were the most sexually responsive woman I ever went to bed with,' he said thickly, not even bothering to conceal his own arousal. 'Perhaps it was no wonder you had an affair. You were always so desperate for it and I obviously left you alone for too long.'

It was a cruel comment, particularly as she wasn't mentally or physically equipped to respond. The intensity of her climax had left her slightly stunned and weakened, but still her body craved more and she dared not move because to move would have been to invite a further caress from his long, clever fingers.

'Did he do that for you?' His voice was hard and his fingers suddenly moved with a skill that made her gasp and arch her back. 'Did he know what turns you on? And were there others, or just him?'

She closed her eyes and shifted her hips, trying to move away from him, but he pinned her to the bed with his superior body weight, his power over her unquestionable.

'Rico, no!' Her own voice was little more than a groan. 'You don't mean this. You don't want this, and neither do I.'

'I think we've just proved what you want,' he said silkily, lowering his mouth to her breast and tormenting one nipple with a skilled flick of his tongue. 'Now it's time to clarify what *I* want. And that, my dear wife, is you.'

She tried to push him away, tried to argue, but his fingers were still deep inside her and the deliberate drag of his tongue over her breast sent shock waves pulsing right through her overexcited body.

Finally she managed to speak. 'You don't want me—'

'No?' His tone was ironic and he moved slightly so that she could feel the press of his erection against her leg. 'Irritating though it is, unfortunately the brain and the body don't always work together.'

'You think I've slept with other men—'

'As I said, brain and body don't always work together. Knowing you're a slut doesn't seem to cure my problem.' His voice was rough and he stared down into her dazed eyes with a grim sense of purpose. 'And at the moment I don't really care about your past. I just have to get past the fact that other guys have enjoyed what used to be mine exclusively. I'm not that great at sharing but I'm working on it.'

Wounded beyond belief, she shot the insult right back. 'And if I'm a slut, what does that make you?'

'Desperate?' He rolled her beneath him with a thickened groan, his mouth coming down on hers with a force that prevented further speech on either part. Sexual excitement, held at boiling point for far too long, erupted with a dangerous force, devouring both of them, sweeping them along in its greedy path.

This time there was no slow build.

No gradual seduction.

The seduction had begun from the moment he'd arrived at her cottage and the time for slow had passed.

He didn't hesitate. Didn't give her time to prepare for what he was about to do. He just slid a hand under her bottom, tilted her to his satisfaction and took her with a hard, almost brutal thrust that drew a cry of shock and ecstasy from her parted lips. He was so big—*she'd forgotten how big*—and for a moment she had to force herself to relax, reminding herself that her body could accommodate this man. Had done so on many occasions.

He paused, a sheen of sweat on his bronzed skin, then he muttered something in Italian and thrust deeper still, fiercely, like a man driven by something other than simple lust. It was shockingly basic. Sex at its most primitive. Totally overwhelmed by the physical reality of his possession, Stasia dug her nails into the muscles of his shoulders and wrapped her legs around him, welcoming the demands of his body.

'Whoever you have been with before, you are mine now.' He thrust again, as if staking his claim, and his voice held a triumphant, possessive note but she was past reacting to anything except the physical sensations consuming her body. She arched towards him, offering more, her movement the instinctive response of a female to a virile, potent male.

'Rico—' she breathed his name, lifted her mouth towards his in blatant invitation and he hesitated for just a flicker of time before lowering his head. And then he took. He took her mouth in a hot, drugging kiss from which there was no escape. He took her body on a breathtaking, sensual ride. But most of all he took her heart, so that when their shared climax finally exploded she held him close, drowning in the knowledge that she'd never stopped loving this man.

He could hurt her, he could infuriate and anger her more than any other person she knew, and yet still she couldn't stop loving him.

She closed her eyes and held him, feeling the thud of his heart, the slick heat of his skin and the warmth of his breath against the sensitive skin of her neck.

He didn't move.

His weight should have troubled her, but it didn't. Instead it was comforting. It was too long since she'd lain beneath him and she closed her eyes and held him, wondering how she was ever going to move forward in her life when this was the only place she ever wanted to be.

The only man she ever wanted to be with.

When he finally rolled away from her and covered his eyes with his forearm, she felt bereft.

She swallowed, risked a glance sideways and instantly regretted the impulse.

If ever a man was in torment then it was he.

If she'd been expecting soft words of love and the gentleness that so often followed on from such an explosive release of passion, then she was doomed to disappointment. There was no gentleness. No prolonging of the intimacy that they'd shared. Only an aura of self-recrimination that thickened the atmosphere until she could almost taste it. Clearly he felt he'd sullied himself by giving in to his own needs and touching her.

Without a word or a glance in her direction, he sprang to his feet and strolled into the bathroom, closing the door behind him.

And then she let the tears fall.

It was symbolic, that closed door. Symbolic of the barriers that Rico Crisanti always put between himself and the women in his life. And she was no different. He might have married her but he shared nothing but his body. She'd chosen to fall in love with a man who kept himself locked away and he didn't need to close a door to create a barrier between them. She'd been nothing more than a mistress with a ring on her finger. *Legalized sex.*

She heard the hiss of the shower running and imagined the stream of water cascading over his sleek black hair, washing the evidence of his torrid encounter from his body. The knowledge that he felt the need to do that cut her to the bone. And the knowledge that she would never be able to free herself of the feelings that she had for him made the pain almost unbearable.

Quickly she turned on her side, curling into a ball

and pulling the sheet over her in a protective gesture. She loved him with a force that would never be reciprocated. Somehow she was going to have to deal with that.

Dio, he had *not* intended that to happen.

Still aroused and despising himself for that weakness, Rico stood under the shower, allowing the freezing water to sluice over his heated flesh. His eyes were closed, his wide shoulders braced against the tiled wall as he attempted to wash away the guilt and shame.

He'd been rough.

No matter that she'd writhed and sobbed in ecstasy. The knowledge that he'd lost control did *not* make him feel good. In fact the realization that he had very probably hurt her appalled him. Whatever she'd done to him, no woman deserved that.

Realizing that no amount of cold water was going to assuage his guilt or the insistent throb of certain parts of his body, he cut the flow of water and reached for a towel.

Why had he behaved like that?

He cleared the water from his eyes and knotted the towel around his lean hips.

Perhaps it was a pride thing, he mused, pacing across to the mirror and registering the degree of dark stubble on his jaw with a frown. She'd left him, so he wanted to show her that he was more of a man than any of her lovers. *That no man understood her body as he did.*

At that thought his fingers clenched on the edge of the basin until his knuckles showed white.

It was nothing to do with pride. He just couldn't cope with the image of another man's hands on her.

On his woman.

Despite the cold shower, beads of sweat shone on his

brow and he cursed softly, recognizing the ravenous, tearing emotions inside him for what they were.

Jealousy. A primal male jealousy that had driven him to take possession of what was his.

But she wasn't his any more.

She'd left and he'd let her go, so consumed by his own emotions that he hadn't even considered a different option.

Was that why he'd been so quick to agree to the doctor's request that Stasia be brought to visit Chiara? Had he subconsciously wanted the chance to take a different route?

He breathed deeply and stared at his reflection in the mirror. From the moment Chiara had uttered Stasia's name he'd known this would happen. There had never been even the slightest chance that they'd be able to exist alongside each other without responding to the white-hot chemistry that had always connected them.

He remembered their first date. He'd taken her for dinner in his *palazzo* in Rome and she'd spent the evening telling him that she wouldn't be staying, pretending to both of them that she was going to be spending the night alone in her hotel room. But her protest had lacked conviction and both of them had known it. Their fate had been sealed from the first moment they'd locked eyes in the marbled foyer of the headquarters of the Crisanti Corporation. Sex between them had had a delicious inevitability that had simply fuelled the excitement and anticipation.

And from the moment he'd discovered that she was a virgin there had been no way that he was ever letting her escape. He'd wanted to keep her. And he did it by offering her the one thing he'd never offered another woman.

Marriage.

He'd given her everything she could possibly have wanted and yet apparently it hadn't been enough and the knowledge left a bitter taste in his mouth.

Until last night he'd believed that there was no going back. Now suddenly he wasn't so sure. He gave a cynical laugh. Which just went to show what a complete fool he was. Even knowing what she was, he was still totally hooked on her.

He splashed his face with cold water and stared into the mirror again, his expression suddenly cold. So why was he denying himself? Stasia was a beautiful woman and she was still his wife. The sex was unbelievably good and, despite her denials, it was still perfectly obvious that she wanted him with the same fevered desperation that he wanted her. So there was absolutely no logical reason why they couldn't still enjoy each other physically.

Wasn't that the best sort of relationship? No empty I love you's. No emotional baggage. Just amazing mindless sex between two people who understood each other.

And when Chiara finally regained her memory then he'd walk away from Stasia without a backward glance. For the final time.

Having managed to rearrange the facts in such a way that he could more than justify a repeat performance in the bedroom, he reached for a razor and started to shave.

CHAPTER SEVEN

WHEN Stasia awoke the next morning Rico's side of the bed was empty and it was obvious from the pristine plumpness of the pillow that she'd slept alone. The narrow sofa in the corner of the room bore all the signs of occupation, the white cushions slightly rumpled. She winced as she tried to imagine the degree of revulsion that must have driven Rico to choose what must have been a fiendishly uncomfortable night over the chance to sleep in his own bed.

Clearly he hadn't wanted to be anywhere near her and why that knowledge should fill her with such a profound depression, she didn't know.

What had she expected? To be woken by a loving kiss?

Hardly.

Loving wasn't what last night had been about.

Rico was a highly sexed guy and he wasn't likely to deprive himself of physical satisfaction just because he had the misfortune to be trapped in his villa with his soon-to-be ex-wife.

She swung her legs out of bed, registered the unfamiliar ache of her body with a wry smile and made for the shower. The long shower he'd taken the night before had obviously worked for him. Perhaps she'd try the same treatment.

Reluctant to face him and having no faith at all in her ability to project the loving front that he was demanding, she took her time dressing, hoping that by the time she finally made an appearance Rico might have finished breakfast and disappeared to his study to work.

She was unlucky.

He was lounging on the terrace looking disgustingly handsome and healthy; he looked like a man who had slept undisturbed a full ten hours rather than one who had snatched the minimum of sleep on a sofa that was most definitely *not* designed to deliver comfort to a person of his build.

She delayed the moment when she'd have to join them by strolling over to the nearest fruit tree. She stood for a moment, lost in memories as sweet as they were painful, and then reached up and picked an orange. It had always enchanted her—the notion that she could pick her breakfast straight from the tree. And Rico had teased her that she had such simple tastes.

She turned the orange in her hand, admiring its perfection. She *did* have simple tastes. But he'd never seemed to understand that. And neither had his family.

Reluctantly she strolled back to the terrace to join them.

Chiara was finishing a sweet pastry and chatting to her brother. She glanced up with a smile as Stasia sat down.

'You had a long lie-in. You must have been tired.' She handed Stasia some coffee and her eyes narrowed. 'Did you have too much sun yesterday? Your skin is quite red round your neck—'

Aware that Rico was looking at her, his long fingers toying idly with his coffee cup, Stasia reached for a plate and a knife. 'I have sensitive skin,' she said quietly and Chiara coloured as understanding dawned.

'Oh—I didn't—' thoroughly flustered, the teenager

stared out towards the sea. 'It's going to be a really hot day. I might go to the beach.'

'Well, take Gio with you,' Rico instructed immediately. 'You shouldn't be on your own. And don't stay there too long. You need to rest in the shade.'

Clearly anxious to escape from the scene of her *faux pas*, Chiara mumbled something, turned a deeper shade of pink and hurried off towards the villa.

Stasia watched her go, peeling her orange with smooth sweeps of the knife. 'Well, I think we can assume that your sister is now convinced that we're very much together,' she said tartly, dropping the peel on the plate and dividing the orange into segments. 'You must be delighted. It all worked out exactly as you'd planned.'

Rico drained his coffee. 'Not exactly. I have regrets about last night—'

'Oh, that's right—' She struggled to keep her voice steady. 'Touching me wasn't part of the plan, was it?'

He tensed. 'Stasia—'

'Do you really think I didn't know how you felt after we made love?' Despite her efforts, her voice shook. 'You hated yourself, Rico. Hated yourself for losing that control that you pride yourself on, hated yourself for touching someone like me.'

He inhaled sharply. 'That isn't true.'

Something in his voice made her look towards him. Their eyes clashed, her breath caught, and suddenly she was remembering every moment of the night before. The heat. The power of masculine thrust. *Raw sexual excitement.*

And he was remembering it too.

'Let's just both agree that it won't be happening again.' She dragged her eyes away from his and concentrated on her plate, wondering if she was ever going to feel like eating again. Even a fresh orange had lost its appeal. 'Unless you're intending to invite Chiara to share our bedroom, there's no point. So you can save your regrets.'

'I don't regret making love to you,' he said, his Sicilian accent suddenly unusually pronounced. 'And the point,' he drawled slowly, 'is that you and I can't be together and not rip each other's clothes off. And don't pretend you were a victim last night. You wanted it every bit as much as me.'

She wanted to deny it. She wanted to wipe the smug, self-satisfied look off his impossibly handsome face. But how could she? When she'd dug her nails into his sleek, muscular back and virtually begged him for more? She couldn't even convince herself so what chance was there of convincing him?

She took refuge in attack. 'You really think you're the ultimate lover, don't you?'

He didn't hesitate, his black eyes burning into hers. 'If your reaction last night was anything to go by, then yes.' He gave a casual lift of his broad shoulders and she licked dry lips, wondering if there was any way she could learn control over her body. Surely there must be something she could do to make her indifferent to this man? She lifted her chin.

'So what do you regret then?'

'Hurting you.' His voice was velvety smooth and as intimate as his gaze. 'I was rough and I'm sorry.'

He caught her by surprise and astonishment stifled the sharp remark she'd intended to make. She'd never heard him apologize for anything before. He had more self-confidence than anyone she knew, a trait that had guaranteed him unrivalled success in business. When negotiating deals he waited for others to lose their nerve—

Suddenly she felt incredibly self-conscious, which was utterly ridiculous considering the intimacies they'd shared the night before. 'You didn't hurt me.' Her voice was croaky and he gave a half smile.

'Good. But if I didn't then it was only because you were as desperate as I was.' The smile faded and suddenly his eyes were cold and assessing. 'So what's your excuse, my beautiful wife? Lover not been satisfying you lately?'

'Damn you, Rico.' She rose to her feet so swiftly that her chair scraped the terrace noisily and almost fell. Goaded and furious that he'd somehow turned what for her had been an act of love into something sordid and purely physical, she turned on him. 'You spent your entire time working. You only came home for sex and towards the end even that wasn't very often. You employ thousands of people. You need to learn to delegate.'

She took a step towards the villa but his hand closed over her wrist like a vice, preventing her escape. Her heart was suddenly pounding at a frightening pace and she met the fierce blaze of anger in his eyes with a sinking feeling. *She shouldn't have said that.*

'When I need a lesson on how to run my business, I'll ask you. And when I need a lesson on how to keep my wife satisfied, I'll ask for that too.' His voice was even but the tiny muscle flickering in his cheek betrayed his fury. 'Clearly I didn't keep you anywhere near busy enough in the bedroom. It's probably only fair to warn you that while we are at the villa you're going to be too exhausted to move, let alone look at another man, *cara mia.*'

'Rico—'

He ignored her shaky protest, his expression revealing a grim sense of purpose as he lifted her easily and carried her back to the bedroom.

'Rico—for goodness' sake—' She struggled for a few seconds but already her body was responding. He only had to glance in her direction and she was lost. She felt the familiar curl of desire low in her pelvis, her whole body achingly sensitive to his touch.

He deposited her on the bed and came over her, pinning her down when she would have rolled away from him.

'You wanted more of my attention—' his voice was muffled in her neck and she cried out as his tongue licked a sensuous path towards her ear '—and now you're going to get it.'

'Rico—this is just pretend—'

'*Not* pretend,' he murmured in thickened tones, stripping her with a skilled precision and spreading her legs for his seeking mouth.

She gasped in shock and then cried out as the skilled flick of his tongue sent shock waves of sensation scorching through her trembling body. He was merciless, exploring her with ruthless intimacy until she hovered on the edge of sexual ecstasy, her mind and body beyond her control.

When he finally penetrated her shivering, desperate body she gave a low moan and he paused, a sheen of sweat on his bronzed features, his own breathing decidedly unsteady. 'Does this feel like pretend?' Perhaps realizing that she was incapable of answering, he thrust deeper, his movements slow and deliberate. If the night before had been crazy and wild then this was slower and more controlled but it was no less devastating. *'Does this feel like pretend, Stasia?'*

He slid a hand under her buttocks and lifted her, thrusting deeper still and then almost withdrawing until she gave a sob of protest and clutched at him, urging him back. But this time he was totally in control. And he took her like a master, driving her to mindless, agonized ecstasy over and over again. And finally, when she'd peaked for the fourth time, he took his own pleasure, driving into her again and again until she felt his powerful body shudder and the spill of his seed deep inside her. He moaned her name, crushed her against him and unbelievably her own body exploded into orgasm once again, contracting, squeezing, drawing him in. He felt it. She felt it. He swore and thrust deep again and again, driven skyward by the pulsing of her muscles and the erotic violence of his own release.

An explosion so violent it had to be followed by calm.

Finally he rolled away from her, drawing his body away from hers and covering his eyes with his forearm. Lying in a state of sensual shock, Stasia risked a glance in his direction, wondering if he felt the same way. If she hadn't known better she would have thought he was lost for words.

But of course that wasn't the case.

As if intercepting her thoughts and determined to minimize what they'd just shared, he opened his eyes and yawned.

'You'd better get some rest,' he advised silkily, springing to his feet with the smug satisfaction of a jungle cat having made a kill, 'so that you are fully recovered for later.'

Later?

Feeling dazed and foggy, Stasia struggled to find her voice. 'We can't keep doing this, Rico—'

'We can.' He spoke with the same assurance that characterized his every move. 'We are, after all, still married. So why not?'

And that was that. To him, sex and marriage were synonymous.

It was truly that simple. The fact that there was a huge gulf between them emotionally just didn't enter into it. The fact that he believed her capable of the most distasteful episode of infidelity didn't enter into it either. He'd decided that he wanted to have sex with her, so that was fine. He was prepared to conveniently forget everything in order to satisfy his rampant desire for sex. It was as if their problems were irrelevant. And perhaps, to Rico, they were.

She was obviously good for sex, and that was all he wanted from her. Stasia stared up at the ceiling with blank incomprehension. Were men and women truly so different? Could he truly experience that degree of physical intimacy with her and feel nothing?

She covered her eyes with her arms so that she couldn't see his magnificent naked body. Her entire body was throbbing and exhausted and yet if he'd turned round and made love to her again she would have welcomed it. And she just hated herself for that. She wanted to be able to lie there and seem bored. She wanted her body to be still and unresponsive.

But it seemed that when it came to Rico, she was insatiable.

It took a few seconds for her to realize that he'd finished in the shower and was now dressed in a pair of shorts and a loose shirt undone at the throat to reveal a tantalizing glimpse of male chest hair.

He looked replete, handsome and extremely satisfied. 'We are joining Chiara on the beach. Can you walk or do you need me to carry you?'

As he'd no doubt intended, the question brought her to her feet with almost indecent haste. 'I need a shower.' She wanted to sound cool and indifferent but it was hard when he was watching her with that penetrating dark gaze that she had always found so disturbing and so erotic.

'Then be quick. I don't want her left on her own.'

'She's surrounded by bodyguards,' Stasia pointed out as she walked into the bathroom for the second time that morning. 'She's hardly on her own.'

'That's not the same thing,' Rico growled, following her and leaning broad shoulders against the doorway.

She shot him a pointed look. 'I'm not showering with you watching.'

'A little late for modesty, don't you think,' he mocked gently, his eyes flicking over her breasts and down her legs with blatant male appreciation, 'when already I know every inch of you?'

She stared at him. 'You don't know me at all, Rico.'

His eyes clashed with hers. 'I know exactly how to touch you to set you on fire,' he said silkily, 'exactly what tips you over the edge.'

She walked towards him and gave him a gentle push, just enough to make him take a step backwards so that she could close the door. 'That's physical stuff, Rico,' she said calmly. 'I'm talking about the emotional stuff. And emotionally you don't know me at all. I'll join Chiara on the beach in five minutes.'

And then she closed the door.

* * *

When she finally walked on to the sand she was surprised and more than a little unsettled to find Rico stretched out next to Chiara in a part of the beach that was still enjoying shade.

She hadn't realized that he intended to linger.

'Not working, Rico?' She sank down on the section of the large blanket that was furthest away from him. Unfortunately it was the only portion still in the sun and she saw him frown.

'*Idiota*—' His voice was rough and he reached out a hand and pulled her towards him. 'You know how easily you burn. Five minutes in this heat and your skin will be raw, *cara mia*. Stay in the shade.'

The concern in his tone and the warmth of his gaze were almost more than she could bear and she had to remind herself that this was all for his sister's benefit. Not hers. Consoling herself with the fact that he would undoubtedly be leaving to go and work in his study any minute, she reluctantly shuffled into the shade, even though that brought her closer to him.

She concentrated on Chiara. 'How are you feeling?'

'Pretty well. Just a bit of a headache.' The girl glanced up from the teenage magazine that she was devouring and gave a rueful smile. 'And I can't remember anything that's happened since your honeymoon, apparently. I'm relying on you to fill in the gaps.'

'Just live in the present,' Rico advised smoothly, reaching across for a tube of sun cream and squeezing some on to his hand. Then he smoothed the cream on to Stasia's back, massaging it into her skin with a gentle, seductive motion.

She couldn't help turning her head to look at him and instantly their eyes clashed, heat flaring between them as it always did when they touched. His hands knew her body so well. Where to stroke, how to draw the maximum response from her—

Stasia bit back a moan of frustration. It was less than an hour since he'd left her lying utterly sated on the bed. And still it seemed that her body hadn't had enough...

'Now I know why I lost my memory.' Chiara laughed, rolling on to her stomach and covering her eyes in mock horror. 'It must have been the sight of you two on your honeymoon. If this is how you are together after a year and a half, you must have been completely unbearable when you were first married. Did you ever get out of bed?'

'Chiara!' Rico's dark brows clashed in a disapproving frown and his tone was sharp. Suddenly he was very much the older brother. 'You will *not* speak like that.'

Chiara sighed. 'I'm hardly a child, Rico,' she pointed out mildly, 'and I do know the facts of life. If I didn't, you'd be worried.'

Stasia gaped in astonishment. It was the first time she had ever heard Chiara stand up to her brother.

'I'd be worried whatever you did,' Rico said roughly, reaching out a hand and touching his sister's sleek, dark hair in an affectionate gesture. 'It is a brother's role to worry. And I have always felt responsible for you, you know that.'

Chiara smiled. 'You have a wife to worry about now, Rico.' She yawned. 'And what I want to know is why haven't you two had children yet?'

For perhaps the first time in his life Rico looked totally shell-shocked. The silence stretched on and on and in the end it was Stasia who answered.

'That's probably my fault,' she said quietly, reaching across and taking Rico's hand in hers. If she was going to play the part then she might as well play it to the full. 'I had a career, you see. A career which I loved and which involved lots of travelling while I painted. I didn't want a child immediately. We decided to wait.'

It wasn't a lie, although it wasn't exactly the truth either. The truth was that they hadn't decided anything. They'd never talked about children. Just as they'd never discussed anything of importance. They'd just fallen into their marriage without looking left or right.

Some of the tension left Rico's shoulders and his hand tightened around hers in a gesture of approval and gratitude. Clearly he thought it was a good answer.

'I'm amazed he let you wait,' Chiara drawled, rolling on to her side and looking at them both with amusement in her eyes. 'I may have lost part of my memory but I do know that my brother is the original primitive male. He wants his wife to produce plenty of little miniatures of himself. If he's let you off the hook so far then don't be fooled. He's just biding his time. He'll get you pregnant any day now.'

Oh, dear God—

Stasia's face burned and Rico frowned.

'That's enough, Chiara.' His words were for his sister but his eyes were on Stasia, acutely watchful. 'You are too hot?'

'No.' She shook her head and managed a smile. She wasn't hot. She was panicking. Neither of them had thought of contraception…

Feeling slightly sick, she did a quick mental calculation and worked out that it was very unlikely that she could be pregnant. She'd have to be extremely unlucky. *Or lucky.* Somehow, despite everything that was happening between them, she couldn't bring herself to feel anything other than warm and excited at the prospect of having Rico's baby. *Despite the fact that their relationship had no future—*

And what sort of a fool did that make her?

Chiara was rubbing sun lotion into her arms. 'You said you didn't want children because you had a career? Don't you have one now?'

Stasia tried to drag herself from the image of possibly being pregnant. 'I no longer paint murals,' she murmured. 'Now I just paint pictures, almost always to commission, so I don't have to travel as much, and sometimes I—' She broke off just in time, realizing with a flash of horror that she'd been about to say that she helped her mother with the antique business. Realizing how close she'd come to revealing the truth that she and Rico were no longer together, Stasia bit her lip and quickly finished the sentence she'd left hanging. 'Sometimes I just like to potter around the house.'

Which wasn't far from the truth. Since she'd returned from Italy she'd been unable to summon up the energy to do anything much. Her little cottage had been her sanctuary.

'I wish I could paint,' Chiara said wistfully, dropping the bottle and lying back with her eyes closed. 'It sounds very restful.'

'It can be restful,' Stasia agreed, 'but sometimes it's frustrating. When a painting doesn't come quite right, it drives me mad.'

'I'd like to learn to paint. I'd like to learn about colour and things. Will you teach me?'

Stasia looked at the teenager in astonishment and Chiara opened her eyes.

'What's the matter? You look really surprised. Did I hate painting, or something?'

Aware that Rico was watching her through narrowed

eyes, Stasia pulled herself together. 'I don't know,' she said honestly. 'We never really talked about it.'

Chiara frowned and propped herself up on her elbows. 'So what *did* I like doing?'

Stasia stared at her helplessly, trying to formulate a suitable reply. The truth certainly wasn't appropriate. In the end she chose to be vague. 'You were a typical teenager,' she hedged. 'You liked clothes and your friends—'

'Friends.' Chiara frowned quizzically. 'Did I have a boyfriend?'

Rico sucked in a breath, his handsome face suddenly like a thundercloud. 'You did *not* have a boyfriend. I was very strict about that. Lots of your friends spent their time hanging around in nightclubs, drinking and picking up men. Fortunately for me, you never saw the attraction of spending your evenings that way.'

Stasia stared out to sea, careful to reveal nothing in her expression. The conversation had moved on to dangerous ground.

Chiara sat up and wrapped her arms round her knees, her eyes fixed on her brother's face. 'So how did I spend my evenings?'

Rico shrugged. 'Studying, mostly. Sometimes you would join the family for dinner.'

Stasia kept her eyes fixed firmly on the horizon. *And sometimes she had such a major teenage tantrum that she spent the evening locked in her room. And on the nights that her brother was away she'd slipped out to a nightclub or invited friends into the house. Unsuitable friends. Friends who Rico had banned his sister from seeing.*

His mobile phone rang and Rico sprang to his feet with a soft curse and cast an apologetic glance in their direction. 'This is one call that I *have* to take. I will be back in one moment.'

He strolled further down the sand and for the first time Stasia noticed the bodyguards positioned at different ends of the beach, intent on their mission to ensure that no overeager tourist or paparazzi intruded on private Crisanti land.

'So go on—' Chiara reached for a bottle of water. 'Now he's gone you can tell me the truth.'

Stasia's mouth dried. 'About what?'

'Well, I may have lost my memory but something about what Rico just said doesn't feel right,' Chiara muttered, rubbing her forehead with her fingers. 'I wish my head would stop aching. I wish this cloud in my mind would clear. It's as if the answers are all there but they're hidden away.'

'Perhaps we should go back to the villa,' Stasia suggested but Chiara shook her head.

'The headache stays wherever I am. I might as well be here.' She glanced at the sea and breathed in deeply. 'I like it.'

Stasia looked at her, unable to hide her surprise. 'Do you? I'm glad.'

'I didn't used to like it, did I?'

Stasia hesitated and then shook her head. 'You used to say that it was boring. But you are older now, and—'

'Less of a pain?' Chiara's tone was dry. 'I had boyfriends, didn't I—and he didn't know. I can tell by your face.'

Stasia froze. How was she supposed to respond to that? Was she supposed to tell Chiara the truth? That it had been one of *her* boyfriends that Rico had discovered that night? That Chiara had been the catalyst that had destroyed their already crumbling marriage?

No. Of course she couldn't say that. Chiara was supposed to be shielded from shocks and, anyway, what good would telling the truth serve now? It was too late for Stasia's relationship with Rico. That was long since over.

All that mattered now was facilitating Chiara's recovery so that Stasia could return home to England as soon as possible.

'I don't think the past is very relevant,' Stasia said finally, giving Chiara a warm smile. 'I think it's the present that matters. And you need to concentrate on getting well.'

Chiara stared at her for a moment and then shook her head with a groan and lay back down. 'I've got this fog around my brain. I know the answers are there somewhere but they're just not clear enough for me to grab hold of.'

What would happen when she finally regained her memory? Stasia wondered.

Rico returned at that moment and sprawled on the rug next to them.

'Why aren't you working in your office?' Chiara murmured and Rico's eyes held a sardonic gleam as they rested on Stasia.

'I am learning to delegate,' he drawled softly and she couldn't help smiling.

'Next thing I know, you'll be talking about how you feel.'

'Best to keep your expectations at reasonable levels, *cara mia* ' He leaned forward and dropped a lingering kiss on her parted lips. 'I'm still a man and men, Sicilian men in particular, do not know weakness.'

She knew he was a man. She didn't need any reminding. With his powerful shoulders, his muscular chest and the roughness of dark stubble on his jaw, Rico Crisanti couldn't be anything but a man. And an incredibly sexy man at that.

'You mean *you* can't show weakness,' she corrected, needing to lighten the atmosphere that was suddenly pulsing with a sexual tension so thick that she could almost taste it.

'That's probably our fault,' Chiara said with a yawn. 'Rico's been the man of the house since he was fifteen years old. We all lean on him and always have. We expect him to be strong and we expect him to always have the answer to everything. If I ever saw Rico looking vulnerable, I'd panic.'

Stasia sat in stunned silence, digesting Chiara's words. She'd never even given his situation any thought. Of course he'd mentioned that his father had died when he was young. And of course she'd observed that he was considered the head of the family. But she'd just assumed that they were a typical Sicilian family. Following Sicilian traditions. She'd never really considered what it must have meant to him to be given such responsibility at such a young age. How could grown women depend on a boy of fifteen?

She glanced at him, her gaze uncertain, suddenly wanting to ask him all sorts of questions that she'd never asked before. Like how it had felt to suddenly be a man when he was only a boy. And who had looked after him while he was looking after everyone else?

When they'd first met she'd accused him of being too serious. But was that surprising?

On impulse she sprang to her feet and shot him a challenging smile. 'Fancy a swim?'

Without waiting for an answer, she sprinted towards

the water and plunged into the glass-clear water without giving herself time to hesitate.

He was right behind her.

She gave a gasp and a squeal as the cold water closed over her shoulders and he laughed and grabbed her around the waist.

'Don't push me under,' she begged, clutching him and trying to keep her balance. 'It's so cold.'

In fact the water was deliciously cooling on her over-heated skin, but she hated the feeling of almost childlike panic that came from being ducked with no warning.

'It's early in the season,' he reminded her. 'The sea will warm up soon. And don't forget that it seems colder because the sun is so hot. If you stay under, you won't feel cold.' His eyes gleamed with wicked intent and she gave another squeal and tried to free herself, all too aware of what he had in mind.

But she was no match for his strength. With an easy movement, he lifted her and then held her suspended while she clutched at him and begged him not to drop her.

He did, of course, and she sank under the water, still kicking.

Spluttering to the surface, she gave a howl of outrage and hurled herself at him. He fell backwards, laughing, and soon she was laughing too.

'Ugh—I think I've swallowed half the ocean.' She struggled upright and smoothed a hand over her face to clear her vision. 'Enough!'

'You surrender?'

'Never.' Her eyes flashed at him but she was still laughing. 'I'm going to wait until you don't expect it and then creep up on you.'

'Is that right?' His Sicilian accent was suddenly very

pronounced and she felt her heart miss a beat as he moved towards her, the water clinging to the hairs of his broad chest.

'No! Rico, not again! I'll be sick if I swallow any more sea water—' She tried to back away from him but her limbs were heavy in the water and he caught her easily.

But this time he didn't try and duck her. Instead he pulled her against him and looked down at her, his thick, dark lashes shielding his expression.

She swallowed hard, her mind venturing back to a time she'd trained herself to forget.

He drew in a breath, reading her mind. 'This reminds me of our honeymoon.'

She closed her eyes. 'No, Rico—'

She didn't want to go there. This wasn't about revisiting the past. It was about healing Chiara and then moving on. And she had no doubt that this playful display was entirely for Chiara's benefit.

'It's a long time since I saw you laugh like that.' His voice was rough and he lifted a hand and stroked her fiery hair away from her damp forehead. 'When I first met you, you never stopped laughing. You were always laughing. Usually at entirely the wrong moment. You were irrepressible.'

Breathlessly conscious of the heat of his body against hers, of his fingers in her hair, Stasia struggled to breathe. 'When I first met you, you laughed too. On our honeymoon, you laughed.'

And no one had been watching.

His hands slid up to cup her face. 'So what happened?'

'Are you asking me when we stopped laughing?' She looked away from him, the pain so acute that it compromised her breathing. 'I suppose it was when we went back to Rome. You were working. I was working. We were both stressed—'

'If you hadn't insisted on working too then the stress would have been less—'

'Damn it, Rico!' She freed herself and glared at him. 'Don't let's start that again! I wanted to work. You knew that. Painting is part of who I am.'

'I never tried to stop you painting.'

'But you never encouraged me. You didn't want other people to enjoy my work. You didn't want me to have any sort of career.'

He frowned. 'You didn't need a career. As you yourself have just pointed out, our lives were very stressed. Your insistence on carrying on a full career merely added to that pressure.'

'So why did I have to make all the sacrifices? You were just thinking about yourself and what you needed. Well, what about what I needed? I needed a useful occupation. I'm no good at sitting around looking decorative just in case you happen to come home for sex.'

He stiffened. 'That is not how it was.'

'That is *exactly* how it was. You married *me*, Rico. You knew the person I was. And yet for some reason the moment we were married you expected me to become someone else. You expected me to fit the mould of the perfect Italian wife.'

'I did *not* expect you to fit a mould. I gave you everything you could possibly have wanted. I provided you with *everything* you needed. Your life should have been perfect.' He sucked in a breath. 'Our marriage should have been perfect.'

She stared at him with frustration. 'What I needed

wasn't material things but you were so self-centred that you couldn't even see it.'

He shot her a look of pure male incomprehension. 'What is the point of landing yourself a billionaire if you then go out to work?'

'For an exceptionally bright guy you can be impossibly dense, do you know that?' She clenched her hands into fists to prevent herself from hitting him. 'I don't just work for the money, as you would know if you'd bothered to talk to me occasionally instead of just stripping me naked on each occasion we met.'

He was staring at her as if she'd actually thumped him instead of just imagining it and for once he seemed at a loss for words.

She glanced around her and gave a humourless laugh. 'Do you realize how ridiculous this is? We've never even discussed this properly before, and suddenly we're tackling the subject in the middle of the sea when it's all too late.' She glanced across the sand and saw Chiara stand up. 'She'll know we're arguing if we're not careful. We should get back.'

Without waiting for his reply, she waded out of the sea and sprinted across the sand towards his sister.

She didn't want to talk about this any longer. What was the point? They both knew that their marriage was long since over. And once Chiara recovered her memory she and Rico would go their separate ways.

And if that thought just *tortured* her, well, she'd have to get used to it.

CHAPTER EIGHT

Rico paced the length of his study, wrestling with feelings that he didn't want to acknowledge.

It was happening again.

Just a few days and he was falling under her spell. It wasn't enough that he had her in his bed every night, he wanted her in every part of his life.

So what sort of a fool did that make him?

Blind to the spectacular view, Rico stared out of the window, remembering the conversation on the beach.

He was not a man given to introspection, not a man given to dwelling on the past. What was the point, when the past couldn't be changed? So why was it that since that conversation he hadn't been able to concentrate on anything?

How could she accuse him of being self-centred?

He worked punishing hours to provide security and a lavish lifestyle for his family. In what way did that make him self-centred? He'd given everything to the marriage. Had offered total commitment, and she'd thrown it back in his face.

Deciding that women were totally incomprehensible, he stared across the garden, forcing himself to review his marriage from a different angle.

Her angle.

Had he really been blind to her needs? His frown deepened. It was true that their relationship had changed once they had returned to Rome after their honeymoon.

He'd been aware of the change but he hadn't stopped to question that change. Until now.

He cast his mind back and shifted slightly, realizing for the first time that he *had* spent a large amount of time working and possibly neglecting his bride. But previous girlfriends had been all too happy to spend their days exercising his credit card and he'd assumed that Stasia would be the same. Instead he'd found her impatiently pacing the marbled floors of his *palazzo*, waiting for him to come home. And then she'd stopped waiting and had started working. And there had followed several occasions where he'd arrived home and she hadn't been there.

He gritted his teeth, acknowledging the fact that he had *not* reacted well to the fact that his wife had been pursuing her own business interests. But then he wasn't exactly a modern guy, was he?

What did she think? That he wasn't capable of looking after her? That he couldn't provide for his own family?

He rubbed a hand over the back of his neck with a soft curse, remembering that night when he'd come home unexpectedly and found her with a naked man in their bedroom.

Their bedroom.

Sweat broke out on his brow and Rico felt his muscles bunch in an instinctive territorial reaction. No, in some areas he most definitely wasn't a modern guy.

But in others—

He paused for a fraction of a second, looked round his study with narrowed eyes and then lifted the phone.

Chiara didn't join them for dinner.

'She has a headache,' Stasia explained as soon as

Rico strolled on to the terrace. He'd changed into a pair of casual trousers and an open-necked shirt and Stasia allowed herself one glimpse and then fixed her gaze firmly on the view across the terrace. Looking at Rico was a fast route to self-destruction because she knew only too well that looking was never enough. Looking led to touching and before she knew it all her senses were involved. Not just seeing and touching but taste, smell and hearing. Her enjoyment of him was all consuming.

She expected him to sit down opposite her, so when she felt the brush of his thigh against her bare leg she jumped.

'Wine?' Without waiting for her answer, he filled her glass and then his own, his hand strong and steady. 'Is Chiara ill? Do I need to call the doctor?'

Stasia shook her head and tried to inch her chair away slightly. *He was too close.* 'She just stayed up too long today, I think. She needs to have a siesta tomorrow.'

He nodded and helped himself to some olives, leaning back in his chair while one of his staff served the first course. 'She is starting to look a little better.'

Stasia found it hard to concentrate. She was just too aware of him. Did he have to sit so close? What was the purpose, when Chiara wasn't even here to see it?

Unable to stand the mounting tension, she rose to her feet, her breathing rapid, her pulse racing. 'I'm not that hungry—I think I'll just go and paint on the beach—'

Strong fingers closed around her wrist. 'Sit down.' His dark eyes swept her face. 'It's time we talked. And you should eat. This mozzarella is delicious. The best. It has a very delicate flavour. My cousin keeps one of the top herds of buffalo. The milk is too rich to drink but it makes the very best cheese. Try it.'

She didn't want to eat and she didn't want to talk but one look at his face told her that she was being given no choice so she sat down again and picked up her fork.

'What's the point of talking,' she muttered, 'when Chiara isn't here to listen?'

'This isn't for Chiara,' he said, releasing his grip on her wrist and reaching for his fork, 'it's for us. I want to talk about our marriage. Being here in Sicily has reminded me of how it was at the beginning.'

His voice was slightly roughened and she knew instinctively that his mind had been down all the same paths that hers had been down. And she knew that he had found it an equally painful experience.

She reached for her wine. 'We should have known that could never last.'

Dark eyes connected with hers. 'Why couldn't it last?'

'Because it wasn't real. When we first met we didn't share anything except our bodies.' Her cheeks heated slightly at the memory. 'We spent our entire time in bed.'

'Not always in bed, *cara mia*,' he teased softly, his eyes sweeping her flushed cheeks with visible amusement. 'Sometimes it was the floor. Sometimes the sofa. Sometimes the beach. Several times we—'

'All right, all right,' she interrupted him hastily, rejecting the images he was conjuring in her mind. 'You know what I mean. At the beginning, our relationship was all about sex. We didn't spend time getting to know each other. When we went back to Rome, suddenly we reverted to who we really were. We were strangers, Rico. And we never got to know each other. You were always away.'

He frowned. 'I reduced my foreign travel drastically.

I slept in my own home more during our marriage than in the ten years before.'

'That's sex, Rico,' she said flatly. 'You always made it home for sex, but rarely for dinner and conversation. Do you realize that there were days when we didn't talk at all?'

He inhaled sharply. 'I was working long days—I had a business to run.'

'Did you?' She toyed with her wine. 'Or were you afraid of intimacy?'

There was a long pulsing silence. 'We were intimate.'

'Sex again,' she muttered, taking a gulp of wine to give her courage. 'You never shared anything with me except your body and your bank account.'

'I gave you everything.'

'You gave me gifts. Money again. With you, everything comes down to money.'

'If it does then it's because I've seen what a lack of money can do to a family.' His voice was suddenly harsh and she looked at him, slightly startled by his tone.

'Money isn't everything, Rico.'

'Try telling that to a woman who has just lost her husband and her only means of feeding her two children,' he said hoarsely. 'Try telling that to a family on the brink of starvation, about to lose the roof from over their heads.'

It was so unlike Rico to be so verbally expressive that for a moment she fell silent, shocked by his sudden uncharacteristic display of passion.

Instinctively she knew he had to be talking about his mother. She was almost afraid to speak in case he backed off, retreated emotionally as he had always done in the past whenever she'd tried to tackle the subject of his childhood and his father's death. 'You supported her.'

He shot her an impatient look. 'I was fifteen. Not exactly in a position to provide the level of support she needed.' He reached for his wine and drank deeply before replacing the glass on the table. 'This is not something I talk about and after tonight I do not want the subject brought up again, but before you dismiss the importance of money so easily you should know something of what it is like to be without it.'

He looked cold, distant, and she sat totally still, afraid to speak in case she said the wrong thing.

'Every day my mother went without food so that I could eat, but my sister was barely weeks old and because my mother wasn't eating herself she couldn't feed the baby. Her milk dried up.' He rubbed long, strong fingers over the bridge of his nose and closed his eyes briefly as if the image he conjured was almost too ugly to confront. 'Every night my sister cried because she was so hungry and every night my mother cried along with her. I started refusing the food on my plate so that my mother could eat it with a clear conscience.'

Stasia swallowed. 'Rico—'

'Do you know?' His hand dropped to the table with a thump and his eyes were suddenly fierce. 'Do you know what it's like to be hungry? I mean really, *really* hungry?'

She shook her head, unable to answer, and he gave a humourless laugh.

'Well, I do, *cara mia*. And so does my mother.' He stared at the food on his plate, clearly remembering what it had been like to be denied even the most basic of human requirements. 'And in the end it was hunger that drove my desire to succeed.'

His expression was so bleak that she wanted to reach out and touch him, offer comfort in some way, but she sensed instinctively that to offer sympathy at this point would be an insult to his Sicilian pride.

'I went to my neighbour, Gio's father.' His tone was flat. 'I asked him for work. Any work. I just needed enough money to feed the family. He hardly had enough for his own family but he gave me what he could and in return I worked for him, although there was little enough to do. But he understood what it means to be Sicilian and to be a man of honour. He knew that I needed to do something for the money. And he knew that one day I would repay him.'

Stasia swallowed down the lump in her throat. The image of Rico as a young boy, fiercely determined to provide for his mother and baby sister, choked her. 'And Gio is still with you.'

Rico took another mouthful of wine. 'Ours is a bond that goes deeper than friendship. My family owes his family everything. Without his father's help, we would have starved.'

But it was Rico who had found the solution. Rico who had laboured to provide for his family. No wonder his mother was so protective of him. No wonder money was so important to them. They'd known what it was like to live without it, to face poverty and starvation.

Suddenly she was ashamed of herself. It was easy to dismiss money as unimportant when you'd always had enough.

'And you have repaid the debt to Gio's father.'

'Many times over, financially. And the loyalty between our families is unquestionable.'

Stasia was silent for a long moment, shaken by this unexpected insight into Rico's character and past. And she was touched by the loyalty he'd shown to his family. *And envious.* Why had she not been given that same unflinching loyalty?

'And your mother depended on you for everything. I see that now. To them you're some sort of god. But I didn't have the same background,' she said simply, her glance a little wistful because she knew that he wouldn't understand. 'The money wasn't what I wanted. What I wanted was *you*, Rico. I wanted to know every single corner of your mind. I wanted to know what made you tick. I wanted to know what made you laugh and what made you afraid. I wanted to know what drove you. And I wanted you to show the same interest in me.'

'I married you. I assumed that confirmed my interest,' he said dryly and she felt her heart flutter.

'Why?' She hardly dared voice the question. 'Why did you marry me?'

'Because once I made you mine there was no question of letting you go,' he replied immediately, his tone possessive and unmistakably male.

'But you did,' she said quietly. 'You *did* let me go, Rico.'

His fingers drummed on the tabletop. 'You walked out.'

'You didn't try and stop me. And you didn't come after me.'

He drained his wine. 'You betrayed me.'

'I was innocent.'

He thumped the glass down on the table. 'The innocent don't run.'

She rose to her feet, her legs shaking. 'But the angry do, and I was angry, Rico. Angry with you, angry with—' She broke off before she could voice his sister's name, reminding herself that there was no point to any of this. 'I can't believe we're even talking about this now.'

'Neither can I.' His voice was thickened and he ran a hand over the back of his neck like a man who was confronting demons that he didn't want to confront.

'You raised the subject.'

'My mistake. Let's drop it,' he growled, 'before I do or say something I regret.'

Stasia stared at the table. She already had so many regrets that it hardly seemed possible to add more. She regretted the fact that she'd allowed the distance to grow between them. She regretted the fact that she'd walked out that day. *That she hadn't stayed to fight for her man.*

She'd been very quick to fling accusations at him, but could she have changed things? If he'd told her all these things about his past sooner, could she have changed things?

Tears pricked the back of her eyes and she heard the sharp hiss of his breath as he registered the depth of her emotion.

'*Not* that.' His voice was rough and he curled a hand round the back of her neck and brought his mouth down on hers. 'You are the *only* woman who has never used tears on me.'

'I'm not crying.' She muttered the words against his seeking mouth. 'I never cry.'

'Tough to the last—' His tongue was seeking, tasting, and they both knew where this was leading.

'Not that tough—' She slid a hand round the back of his neck, drawing him closer, feeling his tension. 'I wish you'd told me all this before.'

'It is *not* something I talk about—'

She felt the warmth of his breath against her mouth

and suddenly her stomach dropped alarmingly. She needed to be with him. *Now*. And the future didn't matter.

It didn't matter that he still believed her capable of doing things that she could never have done.

All that mattered was that she wanted him. That she loved him. When they'd married she'd wanted every part of him. Now she was so desperate she'd take whatever she could get. For as long as it was available. No matter that she'd spent the whole of the past year learning to live without him. No matter that with one taste she'd fallen straight back into the habit, like the worst of addicts.

She wanted him and if the price to pay for that need was going to be high then she was still willing to pay it.

Without shifting his mouth from hers, he rose to his feet, taking her with him, and lifted her into his arms as if she weighed nothing.

'It's fortunate that our bedroom is close, *cara mia*,' he groaned as he negotiated the door and kicked it shut behind them. He lowered her on to the bed and came down on top of her, one hand locked in her hair, the other tracing a path up her thigh and taking her skirt with it. 'You feel like silk—'

'I want you—' She clawed at his back, tugged at his shirt. 'I want you so much.' The throbbing, pounding ache of desire built and built until she was almost begging. 'Rico—'

'I know—' his tone was teasing '—you want me—' Finishing her sentence before she could repeat the words yet again, he jerked her skirt higher still, exposing her trembling, excited flesh to his hungry gaze. 'You don't need to tell me that. You say I don't know you, but there are some things that I know very well.'

She gave a sob and writhed beneath him. 'I don't want to wait—not even for a moment.'

His hands undid the tiny buttons of her top and underneath she was braless. '*Dio*, you are enough to drive a sane man crazy—so beautiful—'

'Now—now—' She was clawing at his back, clutching, just *desperate*. Then she moved her hands to his trousers, trying to strip him but shaking too much to coordinate her movements. 'Rico, now—'

His mouth captured hers again in a hot, sexy kiss and his hands completed the job she'd been unable to perform.

Immediately her hand closed over him and her breath left her body in a rush. 'You're so big—'

'Because I am about to explode,' he muttered, trailing kisses down her neck and trying to move away from her seeking fingers. 'Give me a moment—'

'No—' The evidence that he wanted her so badly simply fuelled her desperation. 'Now. Now.'

'If you say "now" one more time I won't be responsible for my actions,' he groaned, lifting his mouth back to hers and silencing her in the most effective way he knew.

She fell into the darkness of his kiss, floated on the excitement and the promise and finally felt the throb of his arousal against her most intimate place.

Her level of need and desperation was so great that when he finally entered her with a primitive thrust she cried out his name and immediately exploded into an orgasm so intense that she couldn't catch her breath—

Her body pulsed around the thickness of his shaft,

drawing him in, her legs wrapped around him, locking him in place.

Her man.

He'd always been her man.

'Stasia—' His throaty acknowledgement of the violence of her response was followed by an increase in masculine thrust that intensified her never-ending orgasm.

It was as if her body was making up for the long, lonely months when she hadn't had this man. *And for the long, lonely months when she might not have him again.*

The excitement was so shockingly good that she wanted to scream, but he kept his mouth clamped on hers, deepening the intimacy and keeping her silent.

But he couldn't last.

It was all too intense. Too hot. *Too basic.*

Her uncontrolled, electrified response sent him over the edge and she felt his shudders, felt the power in his tight buttocks as he pumped harder, spilling his essence deep inside her.

And still her body held on to his. Even when he rolled on to his back and took her with him they remained joined, their bodies slick with sweat, their hearts thumping in unison.

Stasia kept her eyes tightly closed, shattered by what had happened.

Did she really think that she was ever going to find that with another man?

It happened with Rico because he was the one.

And if she really thought that she could walk away from him and forget him then her brain was soggier than she thought.

*   *   *

As usual he was gone when she awoke.

And it was probably just as well, Stasia reflected miserably as she pulled on a skirt and top and made her way to breakfast. Waking up next to a man that you'd begged was humiliating and undignified at the best of times. Even more so when that man didn't love you any more and probably never had.

She'd never felt less like food in her life, but reminding herself that she was still supposed to be playing a part for the benefit of Chiara, she forced herself to join them at the breakfast table.

As soon as she walked on to the terrace Rico stood and walked to meet her, dropping a gentle kiss on her forehead.

It would have been the perfect way to start a beautiful day if it hadn't been for the fact that Chiara was watching and Stasia knew that she was the reason for the unexpected display of affection.

'Good morning—' His tone was husky and sexy and she felt her stomach turn over.

Oh, not again—get a grip!

He'd made love to her for most of the night. Surely there couldn't be any more sexual energy left inside her? She stared at him helplessly, acknowledging the fact that he only had to walk into a room for her to reach meltdown.

He didn't even have to touch her.

Thoroughly depressed by the realization that she had absolutely no defences against this man, she sat down at the table and then her heart stumbled. In front of her place was a bowl of oranges, still with the leaves attached.

She looked at him and he gave a half smile that made her tummy leap in response.

'I thought I would save you a trip to the orchard this morning.' His smile grew wicked. 'I thought you might be tired.'

She blushed and reached for an orange, unbelievably touched by the gesture and wondering what it meant. 'Thank you.'

They ate breakfast and talked about nothing and Stasia managed two cups of coffee.

Rico was affectionate and attentive, passing her food and making sure that she was in the shade.

His gentleness towards her was all the more poignant because she knew it wasn't real. This was how she'd always wanted their relationship to be. How it had been for those few blissful weeks after they'd first met. She had to remind herself that this display of affection was all for the benefit of Chiara. That none of this was real.

But she wanted it to be real.

She wanted it to be real so badly that it was almost a physical pain.

'Talking of the shade, I'm avoiding the beach today,' Chiara said ruefully, lifting a hand to her head. 'I'm going to have a day indoors.'

'Then perhaps I can suggest something in the way of occupation,' Rico said smoothly, rising to his feet and indicating that they should follow him back into the villa.

Mystified, Stasia glanced towards Chiara but the other girl just gave a baffled shrug.

Rico opened the door to a room that Stasia had never been into before and she gave a gasp of amazement and delight as she glanced around her.

The room looked like an artist's shop. A wide range of different items were piled up on tables, still in the packaging with prices attached.

'Oh, Rico—'

'You say I don't think about you, *cara mia*.' His voice was rough and for possibly the first time in his life he looked uncertain, as if he were struggling to predict her reaction. 'Well, now I'm thinking about you. You wanted to be able to work. Now you can work. And you can teach Chiara to paint.'

Stasia glanced around her, unable to speak.

'I didn't unpack it,' Rico said stiffly, his gaze slightly wary as he glanced at her, trying to gauge her reaction. 'I thought you'd rather do it yourself.'

Stasia stepped forward and picked up a tube of paint. It was the first time he'd ever made concessions towards her painting. 'Where did you get all this? How?'

'I rang your mother,' Rico confessed, 'and then had it flown in. Are you pleased? This room has north light. I remember you saying that it would have made a perfect studio.'

And suddenly she recognized the room. 'This was your study—'

He lifted broad shoulders in a dismissive shrug. 'I preferred the view from one of the other rooms.' But there was a warmth in his eyes that held her captive.

For one wild, blissful moment she thought he'd done it for her. That last night had changed something for him.

And then she heard Chiara sigh and remembered that a change this big must have required some planning and that Rico never did anything that didn't serve a practical purpose.

And in this case the purpose was to convince Chiara that they were a happily married couple. That he was a thoughtful spouse.

The gilt of the moment was instantly tarnished. 'It's wonderful,' she said woodenly. 'Thank you so much.'

He frowned slightly, gave her a searching look and then glanced at his watch. 'I have an important call to make. I'll see you both later.'

Without warning, he pulled Stasia towards him and dropped a kiss on her parted lips but she couldn't respond. It was both a reminder of the night before and a promise of things to come but she couldn't respond.

How much would she have given for Rico to provide her with a studio when they were first married?

And how much would she have given for him to have done it now for her benefit, rather than for Chiara's benefit?

But if it weren't for Chiara she wouldn't even be here, she reminded herself. What with the lovemaking and all the extravagant gestures of 'love', she was having trouble remembering that none of this was real. That at any moment Chiara could regain her memory and all this would be over in a flash.

Rico was still looking at her and his cool expression left her in no doubt that he was affronted that she'd been less than effusive about his latest gesture.

Remembering that she was supposed to be playing a part, Stasia glanced round the room again and forced a smile. 'It's great, Rico,' she said stiffly. 'Really great. Thank you.'

His gaze rested on her for a moment longer, his dark eyes giving away nothing. 'I'll see you both later.' Unusually tense, Rico strode from the room without a backward glance and Stasia watched him go with a lump of lead where her heart should have been.

But Chiara didn't appear to have noticed anything amiss.

'Never thought I'd see my brother so crazy about anyone,' she drawled, strolling across the room and examining some paints. 'And I certainly never thought I'd see him give up his beloved office. This is the best room in the villa, do you know that?'

Stasia managed a smile. 'It's the best. Perfectly natural lighting.'

Chiara frowned and lifted a hand to her head. 'It isn't like my brother, is it? Taking all this time away from work—'

Stasia hesitated. 'Not really,' she said finally and Chiara pulled a face.

'I'm being a bother. Asking endless questions. Trying to complete a mental jigsaw puzzle.'

'No.' Stasia shook her head and on impulse leaned forward and gave the other girl a hug. 'I'm really enjoying spending time with you.'

It was true. The teenager was a changed person since her accident. Gone was the defiant, moody girl who had made Stasia's life so difficult and in her place was a thoughtful, sweet natured girl.

Chiara pulled away slightly, her expression puzzled. 'You make it sound as though we've never done this before. But I lived with you in Rome. Didn't we spend time together then?'

Stasia tensed, realizing that she'd inadvertently stimulated questions that she wasn't ready to answer. Wasn't able to answer. 'Of course we did,' she hedged, 'but we each had separate lives. Now, about this painting—how do you feel about making a start?'

Chiara smiled. 'Let's do that.'

Rico stared at the painting, recognizing the real talent displayed on the canvas.

It had been a week since Chiara had been discharged from the hospital and during that week the three of them had spent a considerable time relaxing by the pool. But he was aware that whenever the occasional business issue demanded his attention Stasia vanished to her studio. And curiosity had driven him to find out exactly how she was spending her time.

He uncovered another canvas and sucked in a breath, captivated by what he was seeing. It was amazing. With a flash of discomfort he realized that he'd never taken any notice of her art before. He'd been too busy looking at her to waste time looking at what she was painting.

He stepped closer, examining the bold brush strokes, the vivid colour. The painting was bright and eye-catching—like the woman herself.

Feeling like a voyeur, he walked over to the other canvases stacked neatly against one wall of the studio. One by one he went through them, his dark eyes narrowed in concentration as he examined each one in silence.

As a collector he knew instinctively that he was looking at something special. As an investor he knew that he was looking at something that would appreciate in value. But as a man he knew that he was looking at something that was part of the woman. *His woman.*

How could he ever have expected her to give this up? It was like asking her not to breathe.

A frown touching his dark brows, he settled the paintings back against the wall and strode broodingly back to the canvas that she was working on at the moment. How could he have thought that marriage to him would be enough to satisfy her?

The truth was that he'd been so obsessed with her physically that he'd given very little thought to her happiness. He'd been putting in long days at the office and he hadn't asked himself what she was doing with her time. He'd assumed that she'd lunched with his family, gone shopping...

But she'd never once used the credit card he'd given her.

When she'd flown back to England to talk to clients he'd been furious. What was the point of having a wife when you arrived home and the bed was empty?

Dealing with the uncomfortable truth that his own behaviour had done nothing to enhance their relationship, he stepped back from the canvas and rubbed a hand over the back of his neck.

It was true that he hadn't wanted her to work. That he'd wanted her to be home whenever he was. He'd hated coming home to the *palazzo* and finding her gone.

Which, roughly translated, meant that either he was an egotistical control freak or he just couldn't bear not to be with Stasia—and what did that say about him?

Acknowledging that he was in serious trouble, he strode from the room and closed the door firmly behind him.

The next few days passed in a haze of pleasure and Stasia was forced to remind herself at regular intervals that this wasn't real. That any minute now Chiara was going to regain her memory and her life with Rico would end again.

But for the time being it was perfect.

During the day she painted, lay on the beach or by the pool. And, even though she knew it was for Chiara's benefit, she loved the fact that Rico had become so attentive. All of a sudden it seemed that he couldn't discover enough about her. He wanted to know every minute detail of her life from the day of her first memory to the moment she'd met him. But if the days were for Chiara, the nights belonged to her and Rico.

Locked in their private world, they made love until they were so exhausted that they slept and when they awoke they did the whole thing again and it was just so *right*—

They were well into their second week on the island and Stasia was quietly sketching on the terrace when Chiara screwed up her face as if she was in pain. 'Oh—'

Stasia frowned. 'Are you all right?'

Chiara shook her head slightly. 'My head feels funny—I don't know why.'

'Have a lie down,' Stasia urged, taking her arm and leading her into the villa. 'The doctor said that you were going to need lots of rest. You probably haven't been getting enough sleep.'

Chiara walked with her without resisting and sank on to her bed with her eyes closed.

Genuinely concerned, Stasia removed her sandals and closed the blinds. 'There. That should help. Call me if you need anything. I'm only on the terrace.'

Then she tiptoed out of the room, acutely aware that her own happiness would last only as long as Chiara failed to remember the past.

Sooner or later Chiara was going to regain her memory and then the whole façade would fall apart.

She was right.

And it fell apart at midnight—

CHAPTER NINE

THE loud sobs woke both of them.

'*Dio*, that's Chiara—' Rico was out of bed in a flash, responding instantly to the sounds of his sister's distress. He paused only to pull on a robe and then sprinted out of the bedroom with Stasia right behind him.

Chiara's bed looked as though a tornado had struck. The sheets had been dragged from the bed and she was sitting in a heap on the floor, shivering, her face blotched with tears and her eyes wild. She looked utterly tormented and Rico gave an exclamation of concern and dropped to his haunches beside her. He spoke softly in Italian, his deep voice soothing and reassuring but his sister flinched away from him.

'Don't! Don't touch me!' She shrank away from him, her brief glance full of accusation before she once more covered her face with her hands. 'You lied to me! Both of you lied to me!'

Rico inhaled sharply. 'Chiara, you are upset, but—'

'Of course I'm upset!' Her hands dropped and her breath came in great jerking sobs. 'I had a terrible dream and when I woke up I remembered. Everything. *Everything, Rico!* Including the fact that you and Stasia haven't lived together for the last year.'

Rico closed his eyes briefly and swore fluently under his breath. 'You need to calm down, *piccola*. Everything will be all right.'

'No. You don't know. You don't know *anything*.' Chiara shook her head and the sobbing continued until finally Rico leaned forward and scooped her into his arms. He settled himself on the bed, holding her in his arms while she sobbed against his bare chest.

Stasia watched in horror, feeling totally helpless. What had induced such a depth of emotion? Was it simply regaining her memory? Suddenly she wished she'd taken the time to find out more about amnesia.

'You have to stop this crying,' Rico said roughly, stroking his sister's dark hair away from her face with a gentle hand. 'You will make yourself ill again, *piccola*. Regaining your memory must be a shock, I know.'

'It's not regaining my memory that's the shock,' Chiara whispered, wiping her eyes with the back of her hand like a small child. 'It's what I remembered.'

Gulping back another sob, she lifted her head and looked at Stasia, her distress both genuine and moving.

Looking at her face, there was little doubt in Stasia's mind exactly which memory was causing the other girl so much anguish and suddenly she felt as though she'd been showered with cold water.

At the time she'd waited to see some evidence of remorse but there had been none. But the Chiara she'd known then wasn't the same person as the Chiara she'd come to know over the past few weeks. And she certainly didn't want her feeling guilty. It was far too late for that. It was time to move on.

Aware that Rico was looking at her with a puzzled expression on his face, Stasia pulled herself together.

'Whatever it is that you've remembered is in the past,' she said quietly and on impulse she leaned forward to touch the other girl on the cheek. 'I think it should remain there and that we should all just think about the present and the future.'

Chiara's eyes filled. 'But—'

'I think we need to get you something for that headache,' Stasia said firmly, straightening and lifting the sheets from the floor. 'And then we need to get you back to bed. Regaining your memory must be a terrible shock.'

Chiara glanced between them, still struggling with sobs. 'You were separated, but these last few days you've been behaving like lovers. Was that for my benefit?' There was a hope in her voice that only Stasia truly understood. She knew what Chiara wanted to hear. That Rico and Stasia were genuinely reconciled and then her actions in the past would no longer be relevant.

But she couldn't give her that reassurance.

Rico dragged a hand through his hair, looking totally out of his depth in the face of so much raw emotion. 'The doctors said that you weren't to have any shocks. When you woke up in the hospital you remembered joining us on our honeymoon. Nothing beyond that point. And you seemed pathetically pleased to see Stasia. To have told you that she was no longer a part of our lives would have been a nasty shock.'

Chiara seemed to shrink. 'I feel *so* bad—'

'That is to be expected,' Rico reassured her swiftly. 'You are still suffering from the effects of the head injury.'

Only Stasia suspected that Chiara wasn't talking about her physical condition.

She tried once more to put the girl's mind at rest. 'You have to stop worrying,' she said quietly. 'Nothing matters now except your recovery.'

'How can you say that?' Chiara was shivering now and Rico rose to his feet with a soft curse.

'I am calling the doctor.'

'I'll do it,' Stasia said immediately, making for the

door. It was obvious that her presence was making it worse for Chiara but, short of telling Rico the truth, she didn't see what else she could do. And what would be the point of telling the truth now? It was too late. Too late for all of them.

Feeling unutterably depressed, she called the doctor and then returned to their bedroom where less than an hour earlier they'd been wrapped around each other, their bodies closely entwined as they slept.

For the last time.

She closed her eyes briefly and then reached for a suitcase.

There was no point in staying. Her reason for being here no longer existed and Chiara obviously found her presence a distressing reminder of her own behaviour.

Not trusting her legs to hold her, she sank on to the edge of the bed and, for the first time in months, allowed her mind to wander back to that awful night.

Rico had been away for a week in New York. She'd been asleep but noises had woken her…

It was gone midnight and she'd already been asleep for two hours. Judging from the giggling in the corridor outside her bedroom, Chiara had sneaked a man into the house again. And Rico had strictly forbidden her to date.

Stasia gave a groan and covered her face with her hands, her brain still foggy from sleep. What was she supposed to do? Chiara already loathed her. If she marched into the corridor and suddenly came on all heavy-handed then their relationship would be damaged even further. On the other hand, she owed it to Rico to at least try and make the girl understand his point of view.

'You're fifteen, and I don't want you seeing boys,'

Rico had told her bluntly only the week before. 'You concentrate on your studies. There'll be plenty of time for boys when you are older.'

'You can't tell me what to do!'

'I can. And you will show respect when you are living in my house.' Rico's voice was lethally soft and even Chiara gave a shiver, knowing better than to cross her brother when he was in this mood. 'If I hear that you have been seeing men I'll send you back to Sicily.'

Chiara's face had blanched. She loved Rome, although Stasia herself yearned for the peace and beauty of Sicily.

Lying there remembering Rico's threat, Stasia glanced towards her bedroom door, trying to decide on the best course of action. She was still deciding when the door opened and Chiara's boyfriend slid into the room, stark naked.

Without uttering a word, he joined her in the bed, covering her mouth with his hand when she would have screamed.

'Sorry about this,' he murmured. 'On the other hand, you are rather beautiful so perhaps I'm not really that sorry. I can see why big brother married you.'

Smelling alcohol on his breath, Stasia struggled frantically to free herself and then suddenly the lights came on and Rico was standing in the doorway, incandescent with rage, Chiara hovering behind him, a smug expression on her face.

'Oh, Stasia—' Her voice held a convincing wobble. 'I tried to warn you—'

Rico's blazing eyes were fixed on the naked man. 'Get out of my house while you still can. You've got two minutes and then you'll be leaving in a body bag.' His voice was thickened and it was obvious to everyone watching that he was hanging on to his temper by a thread.

Chiara's boyfriend needed no encouragement to leave. With a nervous glance at Rico's furious features, he left the bed in a flash and raced down the corridor, still naked.

Rico's gaze was fixed on Stasia, who was lying in the bed shivering from shock.

How had that happened? One minute she'd been asleep and the next—

She never locked the door. Had never thought there was reason to. He must have wandered into her room by accident.

And then she remembered what he'd said about her being beautiful and realized that it had been no accident.

Her eyes slid to Chiara, who was standing behind her brother, and she knew exactly how it had happened.

Chiara knew that if Rico had discovered her with a man in the house she would have been banished to Sicily and that would have been a fate worse than death for the young teenager.

But surely even Chiara wouldn't stoop so low as to hide her boyfriend in another woman's bedroom?

Stasia struggled to sit upright, her eyes still on Chiara, waiting for her to tell the truth. To tell Rico what had really happened.

But she said nothing. And she even had the gall to put a sympathetic hand on her brother's shoulder. He shrugged it off with a growl of rage and left the bedroom with his sister following.

For a moment Stasia sat there, shivering and then her natural sense of justice reasserted itself. She had done nothing wrong! Nothing. And she refused to take the blame for his sister's wrongdoings.

She dressed quickly and found him downstairs in his study, a bottle of red wine half-empty beside him.

'If you've come to talk your way out of it then you're wasting your time.' He drained his glass and looked at her, his dark eyes glittering, although whether from drink or anger she couldn't be sure. 'I don't want to listen.'

'Not even to the truth?'

His long fingers tightened on the glass. 'The truth is that I found my wife naked in bed with another man. An explanation for that, other than the obvious, would need to be extremely creative in order to stand a chance of convincing me.'

Stasia stared at him helplessly.

She was tried and convicted and yet she was totally innocent.

'You don't trust me, do you? After all these months, everything we shared, you don't trust me.'

'I trust my eyes.'

'Use your brain, Rico.' She, who never pleaded with anyone, was pleading with him now. She understood that it looked bad and she knew that she was in an impossible situation. To tell the truth would have implicated his sister and would destroy their relationship for ever, but to leave the truth untold might destroy her marriage and she wasn't prepared to let that happen. 'You know how much I love you. I'm always telling you that.'

His eyes clashed with hers. 'You're also always telling me that you're lonely and bored while I'm away working. It would appear that you've found yourself a distraction, my beautiful wife.'

'That is *not* what's happened here.'

He made a sound that was something between a

growl and a roar, the sound of a possessive, jealous male.

'Get out,' he said thickly, 'while I decide what to do.'

His complete refusal to listen to her sent her own temper soaring. 'While *you* decide what to do? Well, let me save you the effort, Rico. I'm deciding for both of us. I'm leaving you and this sham of a relationship that we laughingly call a marriage. I'm fed up with spending my days just waiting for you to come home. You don't want a partner. You don't want equality in a relationship. You just want a live-in mistress and I'm not prepared to be that any more. I deserve more.'

Without waiting for his response, she turned sharply, wincing as she heard the sound of glass smashing against the door as she slammed it behind her.

Stasia's thoughts returned to the present and she realized that the time had come to be practical. Nothing could be changed now. Too much time had passed.

She'd leave quietly, without saying any awkward goodbyes. Without subjecting Chiara to any further trauma.

And it occurred to her suddenly that she didn't need the suitcase. Everything here belonged to a life that was no longer hers. She would leave the way she'd arrived—with nothing.

Not allowing herself to look at the rumpled bed, the scene of their earlier loving, she found her bag, checked that she had her passport, and rang Gio to ask for the use of the car. Hoping that there would be too much activity in the house with doctors coming and going for anyone to notice her departure, Stasia made her way to the front of the villa.

Although the sun had barely started to rise it was unbelievably warm and she glanced at the sky, thinking numbly that it was going to be another beautiful day.

A day that she would not be here to enjoy.

Gio gave her a searching look. 'You are leaving?'

'It's time.' She managed a brief smile. 'This wasn't for ever, Gio. We both know that.'

He frowned, clearly far from happy with the idea that she was leaving. 'Does the boss know? I think I ought to—'

No. That was the last thing she wanted. Painful good-byes were not on her list of favourite experiences. And for once she understood the reason for Gio's loyalty. Their families were bound by something far stronger than mere friendship. Each had contributed to the other's very survival.

'I need to get going, Gio,' she said quickly, 'and you needn't worry. Rico knows.'

She comforted herself with the fact that she wasn't telling a lie. Rico did know. He'd made it perfectly clear that this scenario would last as long as it took for Chiara to regain her memory.

Stasia slipped into the car, trying not to wish that Chiara had taken a little longer to achieve that state. The teenager was obviously now on the road to recovery and that was a very good thing.

She sat in silence as the car sped through the spectacular sunrise towards the airport, drinking in her last view of Sicily.

She knew that she would never be back.

'It's fantastic.' Mark stared at the painting in awe. 'A bit late, but worth the wait.'

'I had to go abroad unexpectedly,' Stasia said stiffly,

packing the painting carefully and helping him lift it and carry it out of her studio to the front door.

She'd been back for two weeks and she was operating on automatic. She woke up every day and went through the motions of living, but it wasn't living as she knew it. Since leaving Sicily life had lost its sparkle and so had she. She felt like a glass of champagne left to go flat at a wedding.

'Are you listening to a word I'm saying?' Mark frowned at her and she dragged herself back to the present.

'Sorry. I was miles away—'

'It's him again, isn't it?' Mark looked exasperated as they walked towards his car and Stasia gave a lopsided smile.

'I'm a lost cause.'

Mark sighed. 'Well, in that case you're going to be pleased by my next piece of news.'

'What's that?'

He looked over her shoulder. 'There's a shockingly expensive sports car losing its suspension on this track that you laughingly call a road.' He craned his neck. 'I think you're about to have company. Billionaire Sicilian company.'

Stasia felt her heart lurch. It had been two weeks. Two long, torturous weeks during which she'd agonized over what might have followed her departure. Had Chiara confessed? Did Rico finally know the truth? And, if he did, would he come after her?

It would seem so—

She'd spent every moment of every day in a state of heightened anticipation, just in case, and now she stood frozen to the spot as the car approached. Even as Rico uncurled his powerful frame from behind the wheel she still didn't move.

He should have looked ridiculous standing in her overgrown front garden but he didn't. He looked spectacular and it occurred to her that she'd never seen Rico look uncomfortable or out of place. He was a man totally at ease in any situation.

But he wasn't looking at her. He was staring at Mark with blatant hostility, the set of his broad shoulders unmistakably confrontational.

Mark had evidently spotted the same thing because he retreated towards his van, clearly intimidated. 'Right then—' He kept his eyes on Rico, as one might watch a lethal predator who had suddenly escaped from captivity. 'I'd better be off.'

'Good decision,' Rico said silkily, his black eyes flashing a warning that only a fool would miss.

Stasia stared at him in exasperation.

What was he playing at? It was far too late to play the jealous husband.

At any other time she would have invited Mark to stay just to make a point but there was a dangerous glint in Rico's eyes that she didn't trust. And she wasn't prepared to use Mark just to get at Rico. So she quickly ushered Mark into his van and helped him stow the painting safely.

'I hope they like it,' she said quietly. 'And thanks, Mark.'

'Any time. You can call me, you know —' He cast another wary look at Rico and Stasia closed the door hastily and stepped back to allow him to drive away.

'What were you thanking him for?' Rico's tone was icy-cold and Stasia gave a sigh.

She wasn't in the mood for confrontation and one

look at Rico's face told her that she was about to get it by the bucketload.

'For being a good friend,' she said wearily and then immediately knew she'd said the wrong thing.

'How good a friend?' Rico's mouth tightened and streaks of colour touched his incredible bone structure. The artist in her stared at him in fascination while the woman inside her just melted.

'This is utterly ridiculous,' she muttered, talking to herself as much as him. 'You're acting like a jealous husband and yet there's nothing between us any more.'

'You're still my wife.'

'Just a piece of paper.'

'*Not* a piece of paper.' He inhaled sharply and raked long fingers through his sleek blue-black hair. 'If you *ever* walk out on me again without so much as a conversation then I will not be responsible for my actions. That's twice you've done that. There won't be a third time.'

She stared at him in astonishment. Surely he'd *wanted* her to leave. 'I—'

'You are a woman,' he grated, looking like a man at the edge of his patience. 'You are supposed to storm at me and have tantrums. You are *supposed* to express your feelings. You're *not* supposed to just walk out.'

Her astonishment grew. This conversation was not going the way she'd expected. 'You don't express your feelings.'

'I'm a man,' he returned immediately, his tone dry. 'I'm not supposed to express my feelings.'

'So I'm supposed to tell you everything I feel and receive nothing from you in return. Is that it?'

'No.' He muttered something under his breath in Italian. 'That is *not* it. But I used to know everything you were thinking. It was one of the things I loved about you. You were so uncomplicated. You didn't play games. If you were happy you fizzed and bubbled and if you were angry you threw things. And you told me that you loved me all the time.'

And he'd never said it back. Never. Not once.

'This is a pointless conversation,' she muttered. 'I walked out because I honestly didn't think that we had anything left to say to each other. Chiara had her memory back. My role was over.'

'*Not* over,' he breathed, stepping towards her, his expression that of a man with only one mission in mind. 'You should probably know at this point that I have no intention of divorcing you. Ever.'

Her heart skipped a beat and then she remembered what was behind this.

Chiara.

Finally he knew the truth.

Stasia stared at him, feeling totally numb inside. She should have been overjoyed that he now knew she was innocent but instead she felt strangely flat. What did it change? Nothing.

'It isn't that simple, Rico,' she croaked. 'You didn't believe in me. And if Chiara hadn't suddenly decided to confess, then you still wouldn't believe in me. I can't be with someone like that. What happens next time Chiara decides to hide one of her boyfriends in my bedroom? Are you going to trust me then or do I have to rely on other people to confess? Because that hasn't proved to be a very reliable way of clearing my name.'

Rico stood still, not one single muscle moving as he stared at her. She looked at him with exasperation.

What was the matter with him now? Was he shocked because she'd actually brought the subject up? What had he expected? That this was going to be another one of those subjects that they just ignored? Didn't he realize that their problems went deeper than that one incident?

He opened his mouth and then closed it again, as if he was struggling to find the right words. 'Run that past me again—' His voice was strangely hoarse, as if he was struggling with his English.

Stasia frowned. Rico never struggled with his English. He was fluent. 'I was just saying that the fact that Chiara finally told you the truth about that night doesn't change anything,' she said flatly. 'You didn't trust me. And that says it all.'

'Is that so?' His bronzed skin had taken on a greyish tinge and she looked at him in total confusion, not understanding his reaction. All right, so it probably wasn't the most comfortable of subjects, but it was all in the past. Was it really this hard for him to talk about it?

'Rico, we both know that if she hadn't told you then you wouldn't be here now.'

He closed his eyes briefly and when he opened them again they were totally blank of expression. 'I want to hear in your words what happened that night. And I want to hear it right now.'

'And that's why you came here? To hear me tell it in my own words?' Not understanding why he wanted to go over it again when Chiara had already given him the details, Stasia looked at him warily. 'Why now? At the time you didn't ask.'

'I'm asking now.' His tension was unmistakable and she wondered why he wanted to spend more time on a subject that he was clearly finding it difficult to tackle.

'What's the point?'

'Indulge me.' His voice was slightly thickened and she gave a sigh and glanced around her.

'Here? Or do you want to come indoors?'

He glanced towards her cottage as if he'd forgotten it was there. Then he seemed to stir. 'I think we have endured enough head injuries in the family without me knocking myself unconscious in your ridiculous cottage. Let's walk.'

She hesitated and then gestured towards the lane. 'All right. We can walk down here.' She glanced towards him as he fell into step beside her. His broad shoulders were tense and there was something about the hard set of his jaw that made her uneasy. 'How is Chiara?'

'If you'd stayed then you would have no need to ask me that question.'

Stasia stopped dead and raked her copper hair away from her face. 'Rico, you cannot seriously be saying that to me!' She stared at him with a mixture of incredulity and confusion. 'You wanted me there until Chiara regained her memory. And it was perfectly obvious to me that once she *did* regain her memory my presence was making it worse. Clearly she remembered that she was the ultimate cause of our split.'

'Clearly. Now tell me everything. And leave nothing out.'

So she did.

And if she faltered slightly as she recounted the moment when a total stranger had climbed into her bed, then it was only because she saw the thunderous look in his black eyes. Suddenly anxious, she glanced at him searchingly. 'I hope you weren't angry with Chiara. She so obviously regretted it and at least she confessed in the end.'

He stopped dead and turned to look at her, not a trace

of emotion on his handsome face as his eyes clashed with hers. 'She has *not* confessed.'

Stasia stopped too. 'But you said—' She broke off, trying to remember exactly what he *had* said. 'You said that you were here because Chiara had told you the truth—'

'No. That was what *you* said,' he breathed, streaks of colour accentuating his amazing bone structure. 'I said nothing. You *assumed* she'd confessed. As it happens, you assumed incorrectly.'

Feeling as though she'd just jumped naked into a freezing river, Stasia stared at him in consternation. 'No—'

'Yes. Chiara has said nothing to me,' Rico stated with lethal emphasis, a hard glint of anger in his black eyes, and Stasia gave a groan of self-recrimination.

'I don't believe this—' She covered her mouth with her hand and shook her head. 'Are you seriously telling me that Chiara didn't—?' Her hand dropped to her side. 'Oh, what have I done—?'

'Something you should have done a year ago,' Rico said coldly, 'and something Chiara should have done a year ago. And what I don't understand is why she didn't tell me this herself.'

'I thought she had,' Stasia whispered, just *mortified* that she'd inadvertently told him. 'I never, *ever* intended to be the one to tell you—'

'Even though it might have meant saving our marriage?' He ran a hand over the back of his neck and swore fluently, first in English and then in his native Italian.

Trying to remember a time when she'd seen him so close to losing control, Stasia struggled to redeem the situation.

'Our marriage was already on the way out,' she said quietly, suddenly full of anguish but not knowing how to make the situation better. Of all the scenarios she'd imagined, this hadn't been one of them. 'The mere fact that you could even *consider* that I would have an affair showed that.'

'Did it?' He growled the words, his black eyes alight with anger. 'Think about it. You come home early, unannounced, and find me in bed with a stunning blonde. Naked. What do you think?'

She stared at him, speechless, the image he'd conjured so painful she could hardly bear to consider it.

He took a step towards her, his expression grim. 'Come on Stasia, *what do you think*?'

Suddenly her heart was thumping so hard she could hardly breathe. 'I—I don't—'

'You'd think I was having an affair,' he bit out harshly, turning away from her with an impatient sound, everything about his body language suggesting a man at the edge of his limits. 'We are both hot-blooded, passionate people. People like us don't react to a situation like that with cool intellect. You would have assumed what I assumed. You would have thought the same.'

Stasia swallowed. Was he right? Would she have assumed that? 'Straight away, then yes, maybe I would have thought the same. But later, given time for reflection—'

'Reflection?' His voice was a barely restrained growl of raw masculine frustration. 'When did you *ever* offer me the luxury of reflection, Stasia? When? You walked out. *You left.*'

'Because I was angry with you for not believing in me—'

He gave a humourless laugh. 'And I was angry with you for sleeping with another man in our bed. And then I was angry with you for leaving without even giving me the opportunity to vent my jealousy.'

Her face had lost every scrap of colour. 'But you assumed—'

'I *assumed* that you were sleeping with another man,' he interrupted harshly. 'A reasonable assumption in the circumstances, I think you'll agree. And then I *assumed* that the fact that you left me so precipitously meant that you no longer wanted to be with me. That you were guilty. Another reasonable assumption in the circumstances.'

Her pulse was thundering round her body. 'I tried to call you—'

'You left.'

'I was innocent.'

'*You left.*'

She closed her eyes and struggled to regulate her breathing. 'Because I was angry with you, *not* because I was guilty. I couldn't understand how you could think it of me after everything we'd shared.'

'In the heat of the moment,' he said, his tone raw, 'but now, when the situation has cooled, can you understand how I could have thought it? *Can you understand it now?*'

She looked at him, stared into the depths of his dark eyes and switched positions. If she'd found him in the same situation... 'It looked bad,' she agreed, her voice little more than a whisper.

'If you had stayed around then maybe, given time, I would have reached the right conclusion,' he said heavily. 'But as it was you left without further discussion and I was not given the luxury of reflection.

Emotion piled on emotion. My own and then my family's.'

Stasia's legs were shaking so badly she wondered if they would continue to hold her. 'But if you didn't know, why did you come here today?'

Rico gave a twisted smile. 'Because, once again, you left. And this time I decided to follow you. If I'd made that same decision a year ago then maybe we'd be in a different place now. *Dio*—' He glanced at her with a frown and then scooped her into his arms in a powerful movement. 'Your face has no colour at all. On second thoughts I'll risk the head injury. You need to sit down and I need a drink.'

'If I'm pale then it's because you're always covering me with a hat, and I *don't* need to sit down,' she muttered, trying to resist the temptation to bury her face in his neck. 'I'm not that pathetic—'

He ignored her and strode back up the lane with her in his arms. After a few strides Stasia gave up the fight and buried her face in his neck, feeling too shattered to resist. He hadn't known about Chiara. So why was he here? Why had he followed her?

'So if you being here has nothing to do with Chiara, then why did it take you two weeks to follow me?'

'Because for once my emotional reaction to your departure was followed by a period of calm reflection, undisturbed by my well-meaning but interfering family,' he said grimly, pushing open her front door and ducking his head to avoid knocking himself unconscious. 'And during that period of calm reflection I considered a great number of things.'

He sat her down on the kitchen table and planted an arm either side of her so that she couldn't escape.

His nearness sent her senses into overdrive. Suddenly

breathing seemed an effort. 'I thought you wanted a drink—'

His eyes dropped to her mouth and he took a deep breath and drew back. 'Good idea,' he breathed, glancing around him. 'What is there?'

'Wine.' She leaned across the table and reached for a bottle of wine that she'd opened the night before. 'This is the only alcohol in the house. Will it do?'

He gave a wry smile, taking the bottle from her. 'I don't know. That depends on your answers to my questions. I might need something considerably stronger.'

'What questions?'

'About Chiara.'

She bit her lip. 'Rico, I can't—'

'You can and you will,' he gritted, handing her a glass of wine and putting the bottle on the table. 'The time for tact and sensitivity is long past. What I want now is the truth. And I want it fast and undiluted, Stasia, starting with how often my sister invited her boyfriends into my house.'

Stasia took a gulp of wine. 'Quite often,' she mumbled and Rico released a breath with a hiss.

'And you didn't tell me—'

'I was in an impossible position.' She gave a helpless shrug. 'Your sister already resented me—how would I have developed a relationship with her if I went running to you every time she did something I knew you would have disapproved of?'

His mouth tightened. 'So you encouraged her—'

'No!' She interrupted him quickly, her eyes blazing with anger and hurt. 'That isn't fair! I didn't encourage her. I talked to her. I tried to teach her to do the right thing. And she just resented me even more.'

Rico closed his eyes, like a man bracing himself to

hear news that he was most definitely *not* going to like. 'Those nightclubs you went to with her—'

Stasia hesitated, still reluctant to reveal everything, but one warning glance from those fierce black eyes was sufficient to convince her that the time for discretion was long past.

'I didn't go with her,' she said finally. 'I followed her to try and persuade her to come home. If your spies had been doing their job correctly they would have told you that she arrived first and then I arrived after. We weren't together.'

'You should have said something—'

'When?' Stasia's tone was weary. 'When would I have said something? You were never there, Rico. I only ever saw you at night and even then only when the lights were out. We never even had a conversation about our own relationship, let alone anything else. We made love and fell asleep. End of story.'

He tensed, obviously struggling with the knowledge that his own behaviour had contributed to the situation. 'It was a particularly busy time for me at work—'

'Was it?' Stasia's voice was soft and she looked at him curiously. 'I had no idea. I assumed that was normal for you. I didn't know you well enough to know differently. I assumed that you really only wanted to spend your nights with me.'

He winced, visibly discomfitted by her accusation. '*Not* true.'

'But that was what we had, Rico,' she said sadly. 'And I didn't help, I can see that now. Chiara wasn't responsible for the death of our marriage. We did that all by ourselves. By not spending time with each other. My days were lonely and I filled them with work. And, as I saw less and less of you, I became more and more convinced that you thought that our marriage was a mistake.'

'So you worked because you thought you would need an income,' he said grimly. 'After what you revealed about your father when we were in Sicily, I finally understand your need to feel financially independent. But *you* need to understand that I would never have left you without money, whatever the state of our relationship.'

'But I didn't want your money,' she croaked with a helpless shrug. 'I understand now why the drive to provide for your family is so important to you but you have to understand that I never wanted your money. I didn't want it when I married you and I certainly didn't want it when we separated.'

He glanced round her cottage, a strange smile playing around his firm mouth. 'So I see.'

She stiffened defensively. 'I love it. I adore the English countryside.'

'My quarrel is not with the English countryside,' he drawled, a wry expression on his handsome face, 'but with the height of the ceilings in quaint cottages. This quaint cottage in particular. I would rather *not* have to walk round bent double. Which brings me to the other reason it has taken me two weeks to come after you.'

Her heart missed a beat. 'What other reason?'

He gave a frustrated sigh and muttered something under his breath. 'This meeting is not going at all the way I planned it.'

'How did you plan it?'

'I was going to come here, apologize, and you were going to forgive me. Then I was going to give you my present and we were going to live happily ever after.'

Happy ever after?

Another present. Hadn't he learned that it wasn't gifts that she wanted?

She stared at him in silence as she digested his words. She was still the same woman. And he was still the same man. *Or was he?* She frowned slightly. 'You were going to apologize? But you didn't know about Chiara—'

'I wasn't apologizing for that,' he muttered. 'I was apologizing for everything else. Now I don't know where to start. One apology obviously isn't going to cut it.'

She looked at him dubiously. 'Start with what you were going to say before I told you about Chiara.'

He looked at her for a moment and then let out a ragged breath. 'All right.' A muscle flickered in his bronzed cheek. 'But first you have to understand that you were just *so* different from all the women I'd ever met before.'

She bit her lip. 'I was *too* different—'

'Let me finish,' he growled, a muscle flickering in his lean jaw. 'Apologies are *not* my speciality and if I'm interrupted in mid flow I may get it wrong and I'm not sure I can do it twice.'

Despite the emotions churning inside her, she had to hide a smile. That was so like Rico. Always a perfectionist, even in the art of apology! 'Go on, then.'

'I loved the fact that you were different,' he confessed roughly, 'and I loved the fact that you were unconventional. But then we married and I expected you to fit into my very conventional life. And I can see now that I chased away the woman that you were. It was like picking a wild flower and expecting it to thrive indoors. It is not surprising that you were unhappy. I was having an exceptionally stressful time at work and coming home too exhausted to do anything but fall into bed.'

A smile flickered in her eyes. 'You had the energy for some things—'

He didn't return the smile. 'I know that, and I still remember the things you said to me in Sicily. You were right when you said I treated you like a mistress. I did and I'm very ashamed of that fact, *cara mia*. I see now how you could have believed that. But you have to understand that the women I'd known before you were perfectly happy to spend the day using my credit card and the evenings thanking me.' He gave a smile of self-mockery. 'I thought that you would be more than happy to be left to your own devices during the day.'

She smiled. 'Your credit card company must have loved me.'

'You spent nothing—'

She gave a self-conscious shrug. 'I've told you hundreds of times that it isn't your money that interests me. But I didn't know about your work. I didn't know you were so busy. And until that conversation we had in Sicily I never understood why it mattered to you so much.'

'No woman has ever shown the slightest interest in how I generate my capital,' he drawled, a wry expression on his handsome face, 'so naturally I assumed you would be the same.'

She bit her lip. 'We didn't spend long enough talking—'

'Evidently.' He nodded. 'As you rightly said, we shared our bodies but very little else. I learned more about you during these last few weeks in Sicily than for the whole of our marriage.'

'What did you learn?'

'That you are a warm, loving person and extremely forgiving.' He closed his eyes briefly. '*Extremely* forgiving. In spite of the wrong she did you, you came to the aid of my sister. That must have been very hard.'

'Not that hard. She was young—'

His eyes hardened. 'Don't make excuses for something which we both know cannot be excused. I will talk to Chiara at some point but that is not for you to worry about.'

'So that is why you came here?' She hardly dared ask the question. 'To apologize?'

He frowned. 'And to tell you that the divorce is off. I thought I'd made that clear.'

Her heart leaped but she held herself back. 'Nothing's really changed, Rico.'

'Everything has changed,' he announced with his usual self-confidence, grabbing her hand and sweeping her off the table. 'This time I *really* understand what you need and I'm about to prove it to you.'

Stasia swallowed. What she really needed was love. His love. But, as usual, love was the one thing he hadn't mentioned. 'Where are we going?'

'To show you the other reason that it took me two weeks to come and claim you. I was busy.' He looked smugly satisfied with himself and she followed him to the sports car, mystified.

They drove for a short distance and then he turned up a tree-lined road and drove half a mile up a drive to a private house.

He parked the car and they both walked a little way up the drive.

'You said that I didn't understand you, and this is the proof that I do.' He sounded amazingly pleased with himself. 'I know that you love the English countryside but I can't live in a house that is smaller than the average bathroom so this is my compromise.' He looked at her but she returned his gaze blankly.

'Sorry?' Her gaze slid from his to the beautiful Georgian mansion at the end of the drive. 'What has this house got to do with us?'

'We own it.' He made the announcement in the matter-of-fact tone of someone with a bottomless bank account and she gaped at the house and then back at him.

'We *own* it?'

'That's right.' He dealt her a brilliant smile, totally confident in himself and his decision. 'You like the country. I bought you this. *Now* tell me I don't understand you.'

As his words sank in she closed her fingers into her palms and closed her eyes. She could feel him looking at her. Feel the weight of his expectation.

'You are pleased.'

'No.' She spoke through gritted teeth, wondering if there ever was a man as infuriating as Rico Crisanti. Finally she opened her eyes and looked at him. 'If you *must* know, I'm trying to resist the temptation to throttle you.'

Dark, incredulous eyes swept over her. '*Cosa?* It is not to your taste?'

'Of course it's to my taste. It's beautiful. It would be to anyone's taste.'

He gave her a look of pure masculine frustration. 'Then *why* would you want to throttle me?'

'Because you've totally missed the point and, despite what you think, you clearly don't understand me at all—' Her voice was choked with emotion. 'It isn't about the house, Rico. It isn't about living in the country. It's about *sharing*. About making decisions together. About being equal. *That's* what I want. I don't want to be *given* a house, however stunning. I want to choose something together.'

He stiffened, growled something under his breath in Italian and strode off down the path towards the gardens, clearly a man at the limits of his patience.

Stasia sank on to the nearest piece of lawn and just sobbed. They were *so* different; it was no wonder that their relationship had never stood a chance. He just didn't understand the first thing about her.

She cried until there were no tears left and when she finally gave a gulp and opened her eyes he was standing there.

'I just can't get it right with you, can I? I create a studio for you in Sicily, expecting you to love it and you look so hurt that I have no idea what I have done wrong. And I chose the house because I thought you would like it,' he said flatly, spreading his hands in a supremely Italian gesture. 'You love England. You love the country. I thought this was perfect. I'm trying so hard to understand you that it's become an obsession. I am delegating so much at work that my own staff barely recognize me any more.'

She scrubbed her cheeks with the back of her hand. 'Rico—'

'Perhaps you need to understand something more about me. I'm not used to being around women who want to be part of the decision-making process. I'm used to women leaning on me. You didn't lean. Ever since my father died I have been making decisions for all the women in my family. They don't breathe without checking with me first. If I expected you to fit the same mould then it is just because I have had no experience at all of what you are describing. But I can learn.'

She gave another sniff. 'Why would you want to—'

'Because I *want* our marriage to work and I'm prepared to work very hard at understanding you, even if that will mean a steep learning curve. For both of us.'

'B—but I'm not what you want in a woman—' She was stammering now and she just hated herself for being so gauche when she should have been cool and sophisticated. But it was time they were honest with each other. Time to stop pretending and playing games.

He gave a wry smile. 'You are *exactly* what I want in a woman.'

She coloured. 'I'm not talking about the bed bit.'

'Neither am I. Believe it or not, I actually like the fact that I never know where I am with you. I like the fact that I can buy you a house and you metaphorically throw it back in my face.'

She bit her lip, suddenly contrite. 'It's a beautiful house—'

'I will sell it and we will choose one together.'

She glanced at the mansion and then back at him. 'I like this one. I choose this one.'

An exasperated look flashed across his handsome features and he reached out and grabbed her, dragging her to her feet. 'Have I ever told you that you are the most contrary, infuriating woman I have ever met?'

She stared at him, her heart suddenly racing in her chest. 'You instructed your lawyers—'

He ran a hand over the back of his neck. 'I think we could *both* do with being less volatile—that is another part of the learning curve.'

She swallowed. 'I looked hurt about the studio because I thought you did it for Chiara's benefit.'

'By that point I had ceased to think about my sister,' he confessed, tension visible in every angle of his powerful frame. 'I was thinking only of you. And me. And somehow getting back into your good books.'

Good books? Her eyes filled again and he swore under his breath.

'I have *never* seen you cry until recently and suddenly you are doing it all the time—'

'Because you're just trying so hard and it's all useless,' she muttered, wondering why she was suddenly turning into a watering can.

'What now? *Why* is it useless?' He stabbed long fingers through his dark hair, a man at the end of his tether. 'Tell me what I have to do to make this work.'

She gave a hiccough, looking every bit like a miserable child as she brushed the tears away. 'Love me. You have to love me.'

There was a throbbing silence and he looked at her with disbelief. 'I have to love you?'

'That's right.' Her voice shaking, she waved a hand towards the magnificent house. 'This is lovely, the studio is lovely, and I know you're trying *so* hard, but the truth is that I would live in a shack with you, Rico. The one thing I want is your love. And that's the one thing you've *never* understood. The one thing you've never been able to give.'

'Wait a minute—' He shook his head slightly as if he needed to clear it, as if he was afraid there might be a language problem. 'Are you saying that you think I don't love you?'

'I *know* you don't.'

One dark eyebrow swooped upwards and it took him a moment to respond. 'I spent an indecent sum of money on a house in a country with a dubious transport system and an outrageous quantity of rainfall,' he drawled. 'I give up my favourite room in the villa and allow it to be covered in paint, even though you seem less than pleased by the gesture. *Why* would you think I don't love you?'

'Because you've never said it?' Her voice was a whisper and he sucked in a breath.

'I gave you everything. That should have told you that I loved you.'

'Because your way of showing love is providing for your family,' she said softly, suddenly understanding him more than ever before. 'But I needed to hear it, Rico. I *need* to hear it.'

He pulled a face. 'I schooled myself for so long not to say it that it became a habit. I think I believed that if I said those words I'd suddenly be vulnerable. But *not* saying them didn't change the way I felt. I loved you. Right from the moment you challenged me in my foyer. I assumed you knew that.'

She stared at him, her heart thudding. 'I *didn't* know that—'

'Then why did you agree to marry me? If you didn't think I loved you?'

Knowing that she was making herself vulnerable, she hesitated briefly. 'Because I loved you enough for both of us.'

Rico sighed. 'I pursued you as I have never pursued a woman in my life,' he said dryly, 'and I *married* you. Never have I offered another woman marriage. If that didn't tell you how I felt, then—'

'I wanted you to *say* it.'

He tensed. 'I have never been demonstrative, verbally at least.'

She couldn't hide a smile. 'Then get on that learning curve,' she suggested, a note of invitation in her voice, 'because if this relationship is truly going to work then you need to learn to say how you feel.'

'Desperate? Frantic that I might lose you? Willing to do anything to win you back?' He caught the look in her eyes and smiled. 'I love you,' he said huskily. '*Ti amo, cara mia.*'

Stasia closed her eyes and experienced perfect happiness for the first time in her life. 'Say it again.'

He hauled her against him, locking her against his powerful body. 'English or Italian?'

'Italian,' she whispered huskily, her green eyes drifting open and clashing with dark. 'You know how I feel about Italian.'

'I also know what usually happens when I speak to you in Italian,' he teased gently, easing her towards the car. 'And, bearing that in mind, I think we'd better leave before we risk being arrested. That sort of publicity I can definitely do without.'

Stasia followed without question, her body already throbbing with desire for this man. 'Where are we going?'

'The nearest place where we can be assured of privacy.' He reversed the car and hit the accelerator. 'Which is probably your cottage.'

She slid a hand on to his hard thigh and felt his muscles tense under her fingers. 'I thought you hated my cottage.'

'I will be lying flat,' he said silkily, his glance loaded with sexual promise, 'so the height of the ceilings will cease to be a problem, at least in the short term.'

Her heart missed a beat. 'I love you, Rico.'

His hand covered hers. 'And I love you too, *cara mia*. For always.'

If you enjoyed what you just read,
then we've got an offer you can't resist!

Take 2 bestselling love stories FREE!

Plus get a FREE surprise gift!

Surrender to seduction under a golden sun

Why not relax and let Harlequin Presents® whisk you
away to stunning international locations where irresistible
men and sophisticated women fall in love....

Don't miss this opportunity to experience glamorous
lifestyles and exotic settings!

This month...

Cesare Saracino wants revenge on the thief
who stole from his family! But the woman
he forces back to Italy is the thief's identical twin,
Milly Lee. Then desire flares between them....

THE ITALIAN'S
PRICE

by Diana Hamilton

on sale May 2006